DOUBLE TROUBLE

By Harold L. Bare Sr., Ph.D.

Derek Press, Cleveland, TN

Edited by the HGR Editorial Services

Homer G. Rhea, Editor
Nellie Keasling, Copy Editor
Lonna Gattenby, Formatting and Cover Design
homer8238@gmail.com

This book is a work of fiction. Names, characters, places, and incidents are either products of the author's imagination or are used fictitiously. Any resemblance to actual events or locales or persons living or dead is entirely coincidental.

ISBN:

Published by Derek Press
Cleveland, TN 37311

Printed in the United States of America

DEDICATION

To Jesus I owe my greatest joy, happiness, and hope. I was 14 when it became apparent to me that I needed help greater than any human could offer. I knelt at an altar and humbly asked Jesus to be Lord of my life. That encounter has become the singular most important and forceful relationship of my life.

Laila came into my life when I was 18. Our romance was challenging, because she was a driven scholar with an independent mind and no sudden urge for marriage. Convincing her to walk down the aisle and join me at the marriage altar took time and effort.

Laila has been the human driver of my psyche. More than once I would have retreated, but she would say: "Really? I thought more of you than that (my suggestion of giving up a dream)."

I am a man humbly in debt to Jesus, Laila, and friends who have believed in me and loved me beyond my own self-value.

—Harold Bare

ONE

Trouble stood transfixed looking through a safety glass inside the airport. He had just seen the face of a departing passenger. Like a computer, his mind started sorting through images of good and bad people. Bad was quickly discarded.

While Trouble was not given much to emotions, he felt a testing of his spirit that was alarming. His insides were like a thousand nerve endings each jangled by 240 volts. The face that he had seen was a call to another place where love and security prevailed.

Time passed as if there were no clock. He stood immobilized. He liked to figure things out. But there were no answers, only questions.

Like coming out of a fog, he was struck with anxiety. No other passengers or visitors were near him. He was standing alone on a concourse where apparently no flights were scheduled for immediate departure.

Realizing that a young boy alone would be noticed, Trouble turned slowly and surveyed his surroundings. His eyes were arrested by a backpack under a handicap seat. He sensed danger and forgot about security cameras. Instinct kicked in.

Grabbing the backpack, he ran to a passageway with glass walls open to the sky. With all his strength, he threw the backpack over the top of the wall aiming for a space on the tarmac next to a parked aircraft that looked empty. He did not know it was an aircraft used only for training emergency personnel.

Workers at a distance turned when they heard the thud of the backpack. A siren began to wail, and a loudspeaker warned all employees not to approach the object. Dozens of lights began to flash and warning instructions were heard.

Trouble ran toward people. Just as he was merging into the crowd, there was a thunderous explosion that shook the whole building. Shards of broken glass flew, and loose objects were hurled by the force of the blast.

People were screaming and crying. Faces were paralyzed with fear. Voices of leaders could be heard, but not all of them wore uniforms. In times of crisis, leaders are born.

Trouble followed men into a restroom—fear can have a powerful effect on the kidneys. He quickly slipped into a stall . . . took deep breaths . . . and calmed down. He took out the hair coloring he always carried; he rubbed it in, and then changed his hairstyle. He turned his fleece shirt wrong side out for a different color.

He walked out of the restroom behind a man about age 35 who was wearing a wedding band.

Security personnel were closing off all interior areas and pressing people to exit doors. The franticness of sirens, fire trucks, and police allowed Trouble to move with the flow of people. Exiting the building staying near a family, he eased away into the streets hoping to get to one of his hiding places.

He felt like his insides were shaking. Still unnerved by the face of the man through the glass, he was numb when he thought about carrying a powerful bomb only minutes before it exploded.

Having been in the hands of the bad men was elementary to this experience. Sleep came with exhaustion. It was almost midnight when he woke up hungry.

For the first time in his life since his mother died, he felt totally vulnerable.

He needed to be with someone. Preacherman was the only one he could think of. Yes, he wanted to be with him. There was no one else to turn to.

When the body needs food, great issues become of lesser importance. Carefully, Trouble eased into the night and made his way to places where he hoped to retrieve decent fruits and bread put outside businesses after closing. Tonight, he found both good fruit and bread. The quality of foods discarded made Trouble wonder whether the merchants were secretly caring for the poor.

Feeling better and thinking more rationally, he considered where he was and the better routes to Preacherman's place. Normally, making such a trip would have been no challenge, but there was a tension like electricity in the air. Emergency vehicles with lights flashing were passing in all directions.

He wished he had his computer and could search the news to know details of what was happening. But he did not need the news to be confident that the bomb at the airport would cause a state of emergency in the whole city.

His heart skipped a beat as he rehearsed throwing the backpack and feeling the explosion. Then cold sweat broke out on his forehead as he realized that experts would be studying security video. They would see him; they would be looking for him.

He was not concerned that he could be taken as a terrorist. Video would reveal that it was not his backpack and that he had not carried it into the airport or put it under the chair.

Probably his photo had been taken many times, but there had been no reason for police to suspect him or look for him. This time was different. He was involved at a crime scene. He had handled the bomb.

They will have clear photos of me, Trouble thought. *Life as I know it will be no more.*

He was frightened more than when bad men almost kidnapped him at the flat or when water had rushed down a pipe threatening to leave him a corpse.

Subconsciously, he reached for the cell phone that had been given to him by Preacherman.

"You can always call me," Preacherman had said.

It was the first time he had used the phone. There had never been an emergency justifying use of the phone.

Preacherman answered on the first ring.

"Hoping you would call," he said. "Where are you?"

Trouble told him.

"Stay put if you are safe. It is very dangerous tonight. I will come. Do not move until you hear 'Navajo.' Come out quickly and directly to a grocery buggy on the sidewalk."

The phone went dead. Preacherman was fully dressed and had been waiting for the phone call. Cutting all lights, he eased out of his place into the night and to a cluster of bushes where he had hidden a grocery buggy.

He shuffled down the sidewalk mumbling like a man with half a mind, talking like a man with half a mind, and spitting right and left. An old blanket was wrapped around his shoulders giving off a pungent odor.

Crazy folks are avoided by sane people. Not even thieves bother people mumbling weird words and pushing a stinking grocery cart with smelly dirty clothes hanging over the sides.

Preacherman passed police officers and cars by the dozens, but he appeared not to notice them. They did not pay any attention to him other than to give him plenty of room to pass. He was half a block between two main intersections with emergency vehicles and officers checking every car when he paused in shadows and said: "Navajo."

Trouble ran. Preacherman flipped the top cover of the buggy and pointed. Trouble jumped into the cart. Preacherman threw the dirty cover back over the cart, turned around and began shuffling back up the walk. As he spat and shook his head, words tumbled out without sentences referring to Vietnamese battlefields and Huey helicopters overhead.

TWO

The FBI had confiscated video from the airport. After hours without any lead to the boy's identity, a decision was made to release the picture of the boy throwing the backpack in hopes of tips from the public. Hours passed with no helpful information.

Officer Ramírez sat in the morning briefing at the police station. The picture of Trouble was being shown on TV channels of local and national networks. The airport bombing was the focus of every police agency in New York City, as well as many other cities across America. The national alert level had been raised.

Officials were mystified that no record could be found of the boy. No previous photos were useful.

Trouble, in a single day, would change caps or disguise himself with clothes and props. He had a sense of where cameras were and had tried to avoid looking directly at them.

Forensics experts had worked through the night enhancing the airport video, but not one person had thought to do regressive images of what the boy could have looked like when younger. School officials were contacted without any leads.

A well-dressed boy in an airport had to belong to someone . . . a family, probably a wealthy family. That Trouble was an orphan did not occur to them.

While numerous officers admitted to having seen the boy, they could not recall details, nor had they ever spoken with him. There was talk that Officer Ramírez was associated with the boy, but no one could offer any evidence. Truth and legend were mixed with opinions that the boy was brilliant and streetwise.

He had only come to have the name Trouble because of laughing comments made by officers who heard about Ramírez's first verbal exchange with the boy. The story had become a legend. Most officers had never had reason to lock his face into their memory bank as a suspect, even if they had seen him. He was just a curiosity.

THREE

Officer Ramírez had gone to bed early and left home without turning on the TV. He listened to a music station on the radio on the way to work. He did not know about the boy in the video until the morning briefing.

Ramírez knew it was Trouble. His pulse quickened as he struggled to keep his composure. Faking a cough, he exited the room to get a drink of water and visit the restroom. He washed his face in cold water, leaned on the sink and breathed deeply to quieten his inner emotions. He knew in his heart that Trouble was innocent of any wrongdoing.

Having calmed down, Ramírez returned to the briefing and said nothing. His heart was aching with fear for Trouble. Midday, he called in for personal leave and went home. He and his wife drove out to a public park and walked to a bench where they could be alone. There were times of silence and times of intense discussion.

Several times they walked to another bench. As they drove home, a plan was coming together.

Over the next few days, Ramírez made careful and casual visits to every place where he had ever found notes he believed to be from Trouble. In strange and unusual ways, he had received instructions directing him to precise locations. Instructions also included details of suggested body contortions necessary to retrieve notes.

Each place was secret and difficult to access or reach. There were places where he needed to find a rock or object to stand on to feel the hiding places. There were other places where a hand had to reach into darkness and feel for the notes. In a couple of places, he had to lie down, put his hand into a crack, and feel in the darkness for a piece of paper.

In each place where Ramirez had found notes he believed Trouble had left for him, he left a note for Trouble. Now Ramírez and his wife could only wait patiently.

FOUR

Azian was watching the news in a hotel room when he saw the boy in the video. The boy's eyes left Azian with the haunting feeling that he had seen the person before. There was no pause for the TV in the motel room. As quickly as he could, he made his way to the main lobby. The headline story was about the bombing. Pictures of the boy were again on the TV with a caption listing a hotline and requesting information about him.

Azian grabbed a couple of napkins and held them up to cover all but the eyes of the boy on the screen. He had seen those eyes before. They were like Rahel's.

There were no words for such a moment. Azian felt as if he were in a spaceship without gravity and being bounced off the walls. Thoughts of anger toward his father were quickly followed with a rush of emotions, wondering if Rahel were safe. Then came the shock of realizing that the face he saw could be his nephew . . . a nephew who might be in great danger . . . a nephew who could have died with the bomb.

If the boy were Rahel's son, what was he doing in a New York airport? How did he happen to be where the bomb was? Why was Rahel or another adult not with him?

Azian had a frightening thought: *Whoever had planted that bomb had intended for a lot of people to die. A boy had frustrated their plan. They would be angry and want their hands on that boy.*

Never had Azian wanted anything so desperately in his life as to be in New York, find that boy, and make sure he was safe and loved.

He reflected on his sickness in Australia. The illness had interrupted a business venture promising ungodly returns for an unholy business deal. He anticipated the transaction would have been legally edgy, but he had been down that street before.

However, after his sickness in Australia, there had been no further contact from the negotiators. He had no way to get in touch with them. They had promised to contact him.

He knew Azian, while respectful and loyal, had been building connections, gaining respect, and investing wisely and legally since inheriting from his grandfather.

He paused. A shadow crossed his mind. There were other TVs in the house. Servants had access to TVs. The picture of the boy would have been seen by servants and members of the family.

Rahel had been loved by family, friends, and servants. He assumed that when he was not around, there was talk about Rahel. She had been the charm of the house and friends with the servants. Her presence was still felt. While there were new servants, there were other servants who had been part of the family since before his children were born. The nurse that was present when she was born was still an employee—almost like family.

Rahel's room remained untouched, except for being cleaned regularly. Her mother had insisted no one else occupy it. It was as if she expected every day that Rahel would come home. She would sit for hours in Rahel's room with the door closed. No one dared bother her.

Discussion of Rahel was no-man's-land between husband and wife.

Kahlil wondered whether family and servants in the house would see any likeness of Rahel when they saw the picture of the boy in the airport.

He had a moment of anxiety wondering if evening dinner would be served with a lot of silence and side glances trying to read his thoughts. He decided that if no one asked him questions, he would not bring up the subject of Rahel or the boy in the video.

SIX

When Stewart returned from New York City, he had an urgent message from his parents asking him to call.

He felt bad that he had not shared with them about his trip to New York City, but his intent had been to spare them anxiety. He also was trying to make the trip as secret as possible because of the level of international crime he believed could be happening. He feared that family enterprises were involved in ways he did not understand. He was anxious that whatever was happening could negatively impact the reputation of the family business. While honor and integrity are earned long distance, both can be lost in a short distance.

Stewart dialed his parents and began by apologizing for not being in touch. He did not share details about his travels. They assumed his trip was normal business.

"We have news, Stewart," his mother said. "A young man named Azian visited us. He is the brother of Rahel. He shared with us that when she went home, her father was furious about the marriage and locked her in her room. She escaped from her father and took a ship to America. He believes that he knows which ship.

"What do we do? We know you have suffered terribly. We will help in any way possible with personal and corporate resources. Azian believes you could still be in danger because of marrying her and violating cultural traditions."

Stewart was not given to emotions. Logic led to rational conclusions. But at the moment, he was overwhelmed. The thought of Rahel's being alive and in need was more powerful than anything he had every experienced. His heart was constricted, and he could feel beads of perspiration on his forehead.

Out of love for his parents, he controlled his emotions, expressed his love for them, and assured them that he would call the next day.

"I have to have some quiet time," he said, as his voice began to pitch.

He dropped the phone; his whole body was shaking. For the first time in his life, he wept. He could not tell if the tears were of anger or love. Maybe they were both.

It was much later in a *brain-dead* moment, he pressed the TV remote. The news told about the airport bombing in New York City and showed pictures of the boy who had handled the bomb. He was stunned to see that it was the boy who had been on the other side of the glass in the airport.

Stewart paused the TV and studied the features of the boy. Why did he feel so warm on the inside? Why was his pulse quickening? He immediately began thinking of how soon he could be back in New York City.

He was suddenly jolted when it occurred to him that the explosion would have happened just after his plane had left the airport. He had slept, read, and sat in silence while replaying in his mind the video of the boy in the airport.

SEVEN

Captain Syed was at sea watching TV via satellite. He was confident that the boy in the laminated photo he carried was a younger version of the boy on the TV screen. He did not need to take the photograph out and look at it. Long ago he had stored the face of the boy in his mind. If he were an artist it would be easy to draw every feature.

He had carried guilt about not taking greater measures to care for the pregnant Rahel when he had illegally smuggled her onto his ship to New York City. After confirming her death, his guilt had shifted to concern about the boy. He felt compelled to try to find the boy who now could be the person who threw the bomb package over the wall in the airport. How could it not be the boy? There was no doubt in his mind that the boy was Rahel's son.

Captain Syed kept much to himself, fearing that the information about Rahel and her son could fall into the wrong hands. Whatever Rahel had feared, it had been enough for a rich girl to be willing to live in poverty to protect her husband and son.

He knew his emotions were tangled up in the loss of his own son at a tender age. He had adopted Rahel's son into his heart. His mind was often in a quandary trying to determine what to do about Rahel's son. He was grateful for an excellent first mate who could handle the ship and give him private time.

A couple of days later, Captain Syed's ship arrived in Australia. It was not too often that Australia was on his manifesto. He left the ship to his second in command. While cargo was being unloaded and supplies taken aboard, Captain Syed entered the corporate offices of the shipping company.

He had barely introduced himself when a lady executive came up and said: "Captain Syed, we have been expecting your arrival. Our director has requested a personal meeting with you."

"At your service, I am," he responded politely.

"Please come with me," she said in a respectful manner that almost sounded like a command. She turned to an elevator that took them to the top floor exclusively housing the director's suite. When they stepped out of the elevator, Captain Syed was struck by the aristocratic decor. Many of the items were hundreds of years old, with not a few of them relating to ships.

Before he could arrive at the entrance of the office, the door opened. Stewart thanked his assistant and reached to shake the hand of Captain Syed.

Stewart greeted the captain: "Captain, my hope is that you are hungry. The chef will prepare an exquisite meal. Refresh yourself in the restroom in my office and join me for dinner."

They were seated at a table tastefully set with fine china and silverware. Syed had traveled much and knew dinnerware. The set on the table was at least 200 years old and priceless.

The chef received their menu choices and retreated to the kitchen.

While having hot tea, Stewart asked Syed about his ship. It was a subject easy for Syed to share. For a good while, they talked about ships and shipping.

Stewart in an apologetic tone began . . . "Captain, it may seem unusual that you were so quickly requested to come to my office. However, there are reasons of security. I wanted as few people as possible to be aware that we are meeting."

There was a pause and Stewart said: "Captain, though we have not previously met, I am well aware of your excellent reputation as an honest Captain. You are widely respected. Our company has specifically requested on numerous occasions that your ship be designated to carry our cargo. It has been noted that not one complaint has been filed against you for damages, loss, theft, or being late. You have my admiration. Your name bears well in the shipping industry.

"There is an issue of major concern that is plaguing the shipping industry. It involves many companies, including ours. I am certain that not all parties involved are aware of the level of danger.

"Sinister forces are at work. I just returned from New York City. My purpose was to unobtrusively investigate. Oddly, I cannot determine that there is theft. The problem seems be that goods are being shipped without being logged on the manifesto. We are not sure what type of cargo is being shipped without proper paperwork.

"While I was in New York City, significant developments led to the arrest, injury, and death of a number of people at a warehouse. I am convinced that persons at the head of a global criminal organization are hiding behind a wall of secrecy. I fear that there are government and military officials involved. We need help to solve this problem."

Stewart paused as dinner was served. Dinner was fabulous. While Captain's fare on his ship was not lacking, Syed was grateful for superb cuisine without the soft roll of the ship on the seas. Conversation was congenial.

As they dined, Captain Syed found Stewart to be self-effacing and a man of few words. He sensed a deep pain within Stewart as if he had suffered a great tragedy, though Stewart did not even hint of his personal past.

"Well, Captain, how pleasant it is to have good company for dinner. Too often, I eat by myself. How about we relax on the veranda with a cup of hot tea?"

Captain Syed took note that in front of them was a clear glass wall. He was sure from the thickness they were protected by bullet-proof glass.

In comfortable chairs and with tea served, Stewart smiled and said, "Captain, I want to hear about you, your family, your career. As for me, I was married. I was told my wife was dead. There are events happening now that I do not know if my wife is alive or dead. It is a strange time in my life. I want to hope, but I am afraid to."

There was a pause—but not long enough to be awkward. Stewart continued: "Enough of my story. Let me hear yours."

"Your reputation is so pristine. Have there been challenges that have tested your character? Have you ever faced a difficult moment when truth and error were so intertwined that it seemed impossible to be sure what was right?"

Captain Syed began hesitantly to share about his love for the sea, his long career, the loss of his only child—a son. After the death of his wife, his ship had become his home. The sea had become his world; he tended to spend little time on land. He continued as if he had forgotten about Stewart's presence. Stewart listened with ultimate respect, nonjudgmental, intense, yet personal.

Captain Syed remembered the kind words of Stewart about him as a sea captain. He found himself telling the story that had come to obsess, if not haunt, him.

He did not take time to think whether he could trust Stewart. He assumed it. The burden of his soul must be shared with another human being. Too many nights he had lain awake wishing he could turn the clock back and have an opportunity to do differently. Perhaps his failure could find redemption in telling the truth about his one great inconsistency as an honorable sea captain.

"Some years ago, I was in Asia preparing to launch. The ship was loaded. My crew was having breakfast. A person came up the gangplank and approached just as the shadowed darkness of night was giving way to dawn. It was a woman poorly disguised as a man. I say poorly disguised because of her height, voice, and signs of pregnancy.

"Several things were deeply impressive. She was a woman of Asian descent who spoke so excellently that I knew she was intelligent and well-educated. Despite her efforts to camouflage her appearance, it was apparent that she was extraordinarily beautiful. Her eyes were like none I had ever seen.

"But what struck me most forcibly was the absolute terror in her voice. Though she spoke with a controlled voice, fear resonated from her very soul. She explained that I was the only captain she would trust to take her to America. She insisted she knew the other captains sailing at that time and that she would rather die than be on one of their ships. She offered to pay.

"I did take her to New York City, but did not take any money from her. Once we arrived, I arranged for her to stay with a friend who owns a motel. Though she had some money, I left more with my friend for her care and personally gave her several hundred dollars."

Captain Syed poured out his story, trusting. He shared that after a son was born, his motel friend helped to move the mother and son to a single-room flat in a distressed area.

Syed shared about his recent trip to the flat and discovering the woman had died. He told about the boy attending an elementary school, his visiting the school and talking with the principal. With detail, he explained how he had convinced the principal to give him a copy of the boy's picture.

Captain Syed stopped. He realized that Stewart could ban his ship from further association with the family. Stewart could also destroy his reputation, even if no criminal charges were filed.

There was silence. Then Stewart spoke softly.

"Captain, I shall not judge you in this matter of conscience. You did what you thought was right. You may have saved her life. You followed the Second Commandment—love others as much as you love yourself. I would have done the same thing.

"However, I do have a request of you. Do you have the photograph with you?"

"Yes," replied Captain Syed.

"May I see the photograph?" Stewart asked in a barely audible tone.

Captain Syed removed the laminated photo from inside his Captain's coat with a carefulness that spoke of tenderness. It was as if he were handing a piece of his heart to Stewart.

Stewart reached for the photo and held it in his hand. There was total silence. Captain Syed noticed that Stewart's hands were shaking and his eyes were filling with tears.

After a long silence, Stewart spoke. He voice was choked with emotion.

"Captain, I owe you a great debt on two counts. One, you gave my wife safe passage to America. Two, I am absolutely confident that no one could have the eyes of my wife, except my son. I believe the boy in this photograph is my son."

Captain Syed realized that his hands were trembling. He felt as if he were in a cold sweat. Pieces of a tragedy that had long haunted him were falling into place. He recognized that only a greater power could have arranged this meeting with Stewart.

"I am fully persuaded I saw this same boy in New York City only minutes before the bomb explosion. You also probably saw his picture in the news. You have verified that my wife is deceased, as I so feared. Yet, you have given me the treasure of knowing my son is possibly alive. I have hope.

"Together, we have much work to do to find the criminals. But the highest priority is to find my son! It is possible that if we find either one of them, we may find the other."

Silence ensued as they each contemplated the situation. Then, animated conversation began to flow. For a long while, they discussed strategy.

Stewart took Captain Syed by elevator to a private garage. A limousine was waiting to take Syed to one of Stewart's condos in a gated community.

While Stewart had guest quarters, he wanted to ensure as few people as possible knew that he and Captain Syed had met.

They would privately meet the next day to detail further strategy. They had already decided not to use the Internet. Stewart's secured phone lines could be used on a restricted basis. But how and when they would otherwise communicate was the discussion that remained.

They would hold close confidence and only include limited persons regarding their plans.

EIGHT

In a midtown New York City penthouse, the top floor was secured. Bodyguards were generously positioned from the ground floor to the elevator on the penthouse level. The building's owners were in a closed meeting, and TV screens were locked on the face of the boy.

Discussions were intense. Anger and frustration electrified the room as they heatedly argued about the best course of action. A number of their agents had been arrested or killed and valuable property taken or destroyed. Heads were going to roll—whether innocent or guilty.

What had been developed over decades and kept so secret was coming under the radar of investigators. The FBI was asking too many questions.

Adding to their anger was the reality that a box with millions of dollars of smuggled jewels had disappeared. They were convinced if they could find the boy and the Navajo, they would soon have the precious stones back in their hands.

But there was more reason to be concerned than the diamonds. The boy had seen the computers and murders. He knew too much. He would have to be eliminated. The boy had also thrown the backpack, preventing a major disaster that had disrupted other plans for major thefts. Had the boy seen the person who left the backpack? Had he followed a lead from Taj's flat to know about the bomb?

The question was how to get to the boy before the FBI found him. Every available hit man was assigned to find him and try to get information out of him before disposing of his body in a shark tank or acid pool.

Library genealogy records had been searched. Public officials had been bribed to provide birth records and school records. None of the efforts had provided a single lead. The boy must be found.

NINE

Stewart had been in bed more than an hour. Sleep would not come. He leaned against pillows and gazed out the window looking at a full moon. The news of Rahel's death and seeing the picture of the boy had taken his mind to a place from which he did not know how to return.

His phone rang. He answered immediately. Only a few people had the privilege of his private number. He did not turn the light on or look at the dial, assuming it was his parents calling.

"Hello," he said.

"Hi," said Alaina in her gentle voice. "Been wondering how you are."

Maybe it was the moonlight. Maybe it was the lateness of the night and being melancholy. Maybe he just needed someone to listen and the lights were out. Maybe he was lonely.

Stewart was glad Alaina had called. He remembered fondly their brief social time in Canada. He remembered their accidental meeting only because the restaurant had no availability except a chair at his table. An embarrassed *maître d'* had approached him to ask if he would consider allowing another person to join him for dinner.

Dinner and a walk afterward had been pleasantly sociable, but both of them had steered clear of any hint of intimacy in conversation or touch. He had shared with Alaina that he had been told his wife was dead. The conversation had been cordial and polite.

They had agreed to stay in touch. He left abruptly the next morning. Though Alaina was the first person he had felt attracted to, his devotion had been still with Rahel.

Time had passed. He knew now Rahel was dead, and Alaina was calling.

Discussions after midnight can be vulnerable. So much had happened in the brief time since Stewart had seen Alaina, his world was shaking.

Within a matter of days, he had been in New York City and discovered an international crime ring. There had been an explosion and deaths that seemed to have fingers that could involve his family's business.

He had seen the face of the boy who had thrown the bomb package. Back in Australia, he had phoned his parents and heard that Rahel had not died, as he had been told by her family, but that she had fled the family and taken a ship to America.

Then Captain Syed had arrived to share that she had given birth to a boy, and a few years later she had died.

His mind quickly traveled through these thoughts as conversation with Alaina began a little awkwardly. She sensed his tension and mostly listened.

Stewart talked. He opened his heart and shared everything except about Captain Syed. Alaina listened with occasional soft answers, never questioning, often compassionately affirming.

"Alaina, I am told my wife is dead, and that I may have a son—a son who could be the boy who threw the bomb package onto the tarmac!" Stewart paused.

There was silence. Then Alaina replied, "Stewart, I have connections which may be helpful in finding this young boy you believe could be your son. I have resources and contacts with persons in high authority in America. It is quite possible for me to leave in a couple of days for New York. I have business meetings that could be combined with the trip. I do have my own facilities in the city.

"I am a contented person . . . never been married . . . many chances, but it did not happen. I am comfortable financially, and I choose to live discreetly and prudently. The party life has never appealed to me."

Alaina paused and then continued: "Please be assured that my intentions are intended as friendship and an effort to help you find the boy."

Stewart breathed a sigh of relief when Alaina made clear she was not rushing him. He had been rushed too many times. Knowing that Rahel was dead had not opened his heart to a new romance. He had found Alaina's company pleasant and charming, yet there remained vestiges of devotion to Rahel, his first and only love.

He had googled and searched to learn about Alaina. What made him curious was that all information gathered referred to her as a reclusive personality and resistant to social meetings common for her status. There were references to her heritage being of nobility.

He cherished the fact that Alaina had called him. In a lonely moment, he was warmed by her presence over the phone. The idea that she had connections in America that might help him find the boy was welcome news.

"Alaina, it will be seven to ten days before I can get away again. There is something dark and sinister happening in the shipping industry that is bigger than our family enterprises," Stewart said.

Midnight is like a magic wand that can pass over the subconscious. In the darkness with nothing but a moon shining through a window and a pleasant voice over the phone, Stewart continued to talk. He had not shared his feelings since Rahel's disappearance. It occurred to him later that if

Alaina had been sitting in the same room, he would have said much less.

He talked about the first day he met Rahel and how she had dropped her books. When he told about their quiet and private wedding, Alaina exclaimed softly: "How charming!"

He told about going to Australia and suffering months and years of sorrow not knowing what had happened to Rahel and thinking she was dead. He talked about the agony of thinking of her dying and his not being present.

Alaina responded with caring words.

The moon was setting low in the sky when Stewart with deep emotion detailed his shock, grief, and anger to learn that Rahel's family had deceived him. When he shared about Rahel's dying in poverty, his voice was choked with emotion.

There was an awkward pause. Alaina barely whispered over the phone: "Stewart, I am so sorry, but you must now turn your thoughts to the boy!"

TEN

Preacherman and Trouble had not been out of the house for several days. They were like a ship with all the hatches battened down in a hurricane.

News media pursued the story about the boy in the airport and repeatedly played video of him throwing the backpack. That a picture of a minor child was being shown and published left the public assuming the FBI was desperate for clues.

A reward was offered. Hundreds of tips were received, but none identified the boy or indicated an address or family connection. There were reports of sightings, but such information did not lead to specific knowledge of a residence or known social history.

Officer Ramírez and his wife had ideas about Trouble and the Navajo, but he did not speak their thoughts in police circles. He was hopeful that Trouble would find one of his notes. His anxiety increased daily. Whoever had made the bomb and placed it under the bench would not be happy their plan had been foiled.

Ramírez was sure the bad guys had more than one reason to find the boy. There had been a number of crimes that were similar, crimes that Trouble had either witnessed or seemed to know details of the happenings.

While the bomb had destroyed an empty passenger plane and much infrastructure, it had not done the damage it could have done. Significantly, there had been no loss of life, which had kept emergency responders and police on duty in their assigned areas.

Ramírez wondered if the person leaving the backpack had known about the cart with propane tanks parked under the floor. Had the bomb detonated under the handicap chair there would have been multiple explosions with enormous collateral damage and significant loss of life.

Because the backpack had been thrown to the tarmac, not one person had been killed. Most serious injuries were from broken glass and objects falling or being thrown by the force of the blast. A few persons had been injured in the panic of the exit from the terminal.

Execution of such a plot could not have been by a novice or lone wolf terrorist. It had to be the work of an organization—a highly sophisticated organization. How had the backpack passed or eluded security? Did the video cameras show anyone putting the backpack under the chair?

Evidence suggested that the bomb may have been a diversionary tactic for other violence. What could have been done in other locations during a series of explosions? What other crimes had been halted because the backpack had been thrown to the tarmac?

There were chill bumps on the backs of federal agents across America. National security was on high alert. The president was appealing for calm and encouraging the public to call a federal hotline with any information that could be helpful to the investigation.

There was so much that Officer Ramírez did not know. Yet in his heart, he was convinced that Trouble was involved in more than a few of the mysterious and violent incidents. He did not have to imagine that Trouble had thrown the backpack.

He knew it was Trouble.

ELEVEN

Trouble had Officer Ramírez on his mind. He had told Preacherman about leaving notes at various places to help Officer Ramírez solve crimes. Trouble was having one of those journeys with his mind putting strange things together.

"Preacherman," he said, "We know they are looking for me—maybe you, too. But I have a hunch that Officer Ramírez may have left me a note that could be helpful. Is it possible we could visit the places where I have left notes for him? While he has never left a note, I have a feeling things have changed."

They talked and decided that though dangerous, it was worth the risk to visit some of the sites where Trouble had left notes for Officer Ramírez.

Preacherman had night-vision goggles for the both of them. The goggles were a recent military invention that looked more like fancy sunglasses. No flashlights were to be taken on this trip. In addition, it took several hours to dye their hair, use make-up, and select sporty and expensive clothes of dark colors. Preacherman retrieved from a safe two fake IDs with false social security numbers—-just in case.

With lights out and alarms set in the house, they eased into the darkness staying to the shadows for a couple of blocks. Police cars seemed to be everywhere. They tried to find objects for cover or just act like a father and son out walking when police cars passed.

The first few places Trouble found nothing, but it had rained torrentially the night before, which could have washed notes away. There were places that water rose several feet in heavy rains.

Trouble suggested they go to the area of Taj's flat. There was a poorly lighted area near a bridge with a couple of large light poles. It was the outdoor place for taking a leak for those who were homeless, crazy, or petty criminals and drug addicts looking for a fix or quick sexual encounter.

They watched for a few minutes and made the assumption no one was in the area. Preacherman found a good place to observe and be ready for quick action.

Trouble took a deep breath and stepped into the semi-darkness of the hole, hoping he could hold his breath. The stench was awful. Even in his darkest moments of being homeless, he had found a way to bathe and wear clean clothes. Poor is no excuse for being dirty when there is water.

Trouble closed his eyes. Night-vision goggles cannot see around a blind corner. He felt with his mind as his hand went behind a pole and moved up the wall of a bridge abutment searching for an age crack. His fingers found the crevice and moved left to right. He was concentrating intensely when a series of gunshots sounded—too close for comfort. His heart was beating frantically.

At that same moment, his fingers felt paper. He carefully retracted the paper, making certain not to drop it. He then retreated quickly to a safe area to take a deep breath of fresh air. Securing the paper in a zipped pocket, he eased through the shadows to stand immobile beside Preacherman and whisper: "I have a note."

"Then, my boy, I suggest we light a shuck out of here. This place is giving me the heebie-jeebies like a Viet Cong minefield."

Police cars were coming from every direction with lights flashing and sirens blaring. Whether gang warfare or another crime, this was not the place to be.

If Preacherman had saved Trouble's hide a few times, turnabout was fair play. Trouble knew a thing or two about this part of the city that Preacherman did not know. Preacherman had lived with combat skills and the cunning of a Navajo warrior. Trouble's life before Preacherman had depended upon intellect and ingenuity. Trouble led them through a series of narrow passages, across roofs, and through pipes until they could no longer hear sirens.

Both breathed a sigh of relief when they stepped into Preacherman's house and heard the click of the door latching and the buzz indicating the security system was fully functional.

The piece of paper found in the crevice was unfolded carefully and placed on the table.

Officer Ramírez had written: "Can we talk? I have information that may be helpful to you. Come to my home at 1 a.m. Sunday morning with the man who has been a protector for you. My wife and I live alone in a gated community. I will post security at the gate that family are arriving.

"Bring suitcases to give the illusion you are family who have traveled some distance, in the event anyone would happen to see you. Use gate code Family B14. It would be best if you come by taxi."

It was signed 'OR.'

Perhaps it was the pressure of the moment. Perhaps it was the innate sense of human beings believing in the goodness of other human beings. With great relief, Trouble and Preacherman began planning for the Sunday meeting with Ramírez and his wife.

They would not go unprepared. The suitcases Officer Ramírez had suggested would have enough ammunition and firepower to wage a small-scale war—just in case.

They had no intention of falling into the hands of bad men or police officers. Neither had ever experienced handcuffs, and they did not intend on this adventure to be initiated in the backseat of a police cruiser.

TWELVE

Syed left his meeting with Stewart knowing there would be challenges ahead. Bad people were aware of his knowledge of Rahel's son being alive. The boy would be in imminent danger with video of him throwing the bomb onto the tarmac. And anyone who was close to the boy would be in danger, including Syed.

Syed had been thinking of retiring. There was always an offer on the table from a purchaser. Only the love for his ship and the sea had prevented him from selling. The ship had been custom-designed by a Dutch builder with Syed adding personal touches. Heads turned when Syed's ship passed.

Syed had no kin to inherit his ship or investments—a diversified portfolio thoughtfully invested in numerous countries. The ship was his life, his heartbeat, except that he now thought more often of Rahel's son than his ship.

He arranged for a shipment of food supplies to be delivered to Israel, a port he had not been to for years. Negotiating through private and trusted friends, he scheduled for a maintenance service of his ship. Not represented in the paperwork was a lot of cash he had included to install fancy upgrades. Speed and the maneuver would be greatly increased.

The crew had been given paid leave in Tel Aviv. No one objected. While they were off the ship twenty-four hours per day, workmen were modifying and creating secret areas with panels electronically controlled. Guns were installed that could be remotely operated from the Captain's deck.

When Syed's crew returned, the ship did not look much different except for fancy painting. There were a few rule changes, including restrictions to certain areas of the ship. He did not want the rest of the crew to know about the new engines which were sleek, beautiful, and the most powerful in the world for ships of similar size.

In a stroke of genius, Syed had asked the engineers to design ballasts on either side of the ship. The ballasts were aero-engineered. Pumps could fill them with air, lifting the ship and allowing greater speed.

Syed wistfully smiled to himself. It would be doubtful if another ship of common size could outmaneuver or even dream of the speed of his ship. The cost had been high, but he was pleased. His investments had returned great dividends, and he could afford the expense. It was not splurging, but investing. Even with the high cost, his portfolio was impressive.

They sailed out of the Tel Aviv harbor with a light load of computers and technological machines to be delivered to Rangoon Harbor, Myanmar. Everything seemed normal when they arrived at their destination and eased into a berth between two Asian ships.

As was his custom in new harbors, Captain Syed forbade any shore leave until cargo was unloaded. Without others knowing, he slipped to his observation room where he could observe his own ship and surrounding ships. The one-way smoked glass windows prevented others from being aware of his presence.

Just after 2 a.m., he came alert as he observed men moving objects onto an adjacent ship. Why would they not be using lights? Why would they be moving objects onto the ship in the middle of the night? What objects were being transported that were bypassing customs? Or had customs been bribed?

One of Captain Syed's crewmembers at that moment accidentally swung a powerful search light in the direction of the ship in question. Suddenly Captain Syed's ship was flooded with blinding lights. Just as quickly, the lights went off leaving total darkness.

It was unnerving. Captain Syed spoke into the microphone to each station quietly asking them to be on special alert.

While he was thinking about what to do next, the other ship eased away from the harbor into deeper waters. Syed puzzled that a ship would move in almost total darkness, but then it occurred to him that the ship had done this many times before.

When daylight came, the ship was gone . . . as he knew it would be.

Captain Syed had a bad feeling about the night incident. Why had they flooded his ship with light? To blind his men? To intimidate? To threaten? Or had it been to identify his ship and take pictures? Why had the ship moved out of the harbor toward the bay?

It did not feel right. With a chill in his bones, he shuddered, knowing their ships would meet again.

THIRTEEN

Alaina arrived in New York by private jet at a private airport. This trip was to be as quiet as possible. While she owned U.S. residences, she had made arrangements for a 90-day lease of an estate on Long Island.

The next morning she thought to call Jeb who was a friend several years younger. He had been 18 years old and employed by an affiliate of her enterprises when a crazy Friday night turned into a nightmare. Out with friends, Jeb was involved in an accident, resulting in a person being killed. Unknown to Jeb, one of his friends was carrying several ounces of cocaine. Jeb was drawn into a threatening situation that could have resulted in jail time and ruined hopes of college and a career.

Alaina had come to his rescue. She believed in Jeb and hired excellent lawyers. All charges were dismissed.

Jeb had proceeded to college, studied criminology and become a Secret Service agent. A friendship with Alaina had remained strong. Jeb had married his childhood sweetheart, and the both of them stayed in touch with Alaina.

She called Jeb the next morning and asked if he could come with his wife and visit. She asked that they not share about her presence in the United States.

The three of them had dinner that evening. Alaina did not need to inform Jeb about the airport bomb and the boy. She did share about Stewart and the thought that the boy could be Stewart's son.

"Jeb, I am not asking you to do anything illegal or that would risk your future. But I am asking you to think about your connections and how efforts can be made to find the boy. We believe he is in danger."

Jeb asked many questions before he and his wife left.

FOURTEEN

Azian was staying in touch with Stewart's parents, but he had no further information about Rahel's son. He did share that he was sensing a change in Kahlil, his father.

He wondered if Kahlil was regretting his treatment of Rahel. He knew that his father puzzled about his mysterious travels. Not being able to trace him in his travels frustrated his father. There was a coolness and distance between them.

His father was intelligent and would notice Azian's travels were not random. There was a pattern to the travels, and the eyes of his father's agents would be figuring out the pattern.

The absence of Rahel had created ghosts in the household. Suspense hung in the air. Rahel had been a living presence. Everyone in the family and many servants had come to know she was pregnant when she disappeared. Her maid had found evidence in Rahel's room of her pregnancy and shared it with the other workers. What other mysteries had been circulated?

Azian decided to ask Stewart's parents for permission to phone Stewart. They agreed to the idea and gave him codes to access a secure line.

Stewart was delighted to hear from Azian. Rahel had told him about her brother. Talking to Azian refreshed memories of Rahel. Their conversation was long, both sharing whatever information they had about Rahel's disappearance, trip to New York, her death, and the possibility of the boy in the airport being Stewart's son.

Stewart shared about Alaina and her trip to the United

States to assist in efforts to find the boy and his intentions to leave for America within a few days. He and Azian exchanged phone numbers and agreed to stay in touch.

FIFTEEN

Officer Ramírez was intrigued by his wife's cheerfulness and excitement. She had spent much of the day in the kitchen producing a superb meal and delicacies that had not been baked in their home in years.

The wisdom of silence is often the best testimony of a good husband. She was a strong woman. He had to be grateful for her insights and counsel that had brought about the hope of meeting Trouble.

Not long after midnight, the doorbell rang. Ramírez had installed a low-wattage bulb in the porch light that would make it difficult for neighbors to see more than figures carrying suitcases. He opened the door, graciously greeted Preacherman and Trouble and invited them in. Shades had been pulled.

They set their suitcases down near them and accepted glasses of water. Mrs. Ramírez started bringing food to a small table that had been set up for the occasion. Her charm, graciousness, and the aroma of the food calmed the atmosphere. Preacherman and Trouble felt secure and relaxed.

Officer Ramírez began the conversation by thanking them for coming. He explained that he would prefer they not share any details with him. Rather, he wanted to inform them of things he knew that were possibly dangerous for them.

He shared that Trouble's picture was posted in police stations across the city and possibly across the country. There was a national effort among law enforcement to locate the boy. Ramírez was confident that local, state, and federal agents were focused on finding Trouble to interview him and to protect him.

Removing the tags and lettering from the van and making sure it was wiped down of fingerprints and impeccably clean, they followed Preacherman's instructions and left an envelope with $1,000 cash in the mailbox on the church doors.

They eased into the morning shadows to a nearby railroad and "hoboed" a train going west.

The third Navajo drove Preacherman and Trouble across the reservation without stopping. More than once, the vehicle left the road and crossed rough terrain to make sure no vehicle was following them. When off-road, a heavy flap was dragged behind the vehicle to erase tire marks.

Their presence on the reservation was a secret that would be intensely guarded. The destination was an uninhabited remote corner of the reservation with only primitive roads and no electricity.

A cave had been prepared with generators, food, and necessary items. It would be a mix of modern-day camping and primitive living.

A band of trusted warriors, several of whom were veterans with skills in communications had taken the area off-the-grid. There were no known tools of mankind that could penetrate a ten-mile perimeter to send or receive an electronic message. Humans would transport all communications, depending totally on memory.

The area was so remote that no one imagined it to be habitable or a hiding place. The truck was driven under the ledge of a rock overhang. Within a few hours, stones had been laid up as a wall hiding the truck from the outside world. The best of an aerial photograph would not have detected anything different about the landscape than was present a thousand years ago.

Warriors were placed strategically for miles surrounding the site and across the reservation. There were other warriors strategically imbedded in the communities across the Navajo Nation to listen and watch. Movement in the main camp would be kept to a minimum during daytime.

Weapons ranged from primitive to the most modern, having been obtained from numerous countries. Many of the weapons had been customized or modified to be more efficient and more powerful.

But to the native Indian, the mind is the greatest weapon. Every man present was bound to a mission with multiple purposes. Preacherman and Trouble were their blood brothers. The world had become small to them. They no longer cared about wars in distant places. Their duty to country had been done. This was personal. This was their battlefield. They were Navajo.

Preacherman and Trouble needed their help. There were precious stones to be sold. Half of the proceeds would serve to improve living conditions on the reservation. If they succeeded in black-marketing the diamonds, there would be water lines run to hundreds of homes on the reservation.

An international network had been established. Navajo Indians would carry the diamonds off the reservation to contact persons across the United States and in other countries. Layers of security had been carefully developed that would make it incredibly difficult, if not impossible, to trace the origin of the diamonds.

Dealing with the sale of stones was Preacherman's task. Estimates were that black-market value could be between $18 and $22 million.

Trouble's challenge was personal. His young body was wiry and strong. He needed muscle and bulk. There would be times that his mind would need physical force.

His days of living in culverts and secret places were over.

Law enforcement was desperately looking for both of them in relation to the airport bombing and subsequent explosions, including Preacherman's home. No bodies or parts of bodies had been found in the devastation of the home.

Of greater concern to Preacherman and Trouble was the awareness that a syndicate knew the two of them were connected. Missing diamonds would bring the wrath of hell. There was a string of bodies and cars left in shards of metal, and millions of dollars of contraband confiscated by police.

Trouble's face was known to the cartel. He had been seen via camera in the flat. Pictures of him at the airport would leave no doubt that he was the same person they had almost kidnapped.

What puzzled the cartel was how Trouble had known about the backpack. Did he have inside information? Was he aware of who had left the backpack? What else did he know? How could a boy know about the bomb and throw it to the tarmac?

The cartel had carefully planned the airport bombing as a distraction. Two banks—one of them a Federal Reserve—a wholesale jeweler, and an office with machines to print driver's licenses had been targets frustrated by the boy in the airport throwing the bomb. Had there been scores of deaths, police and emergency vehicles would have been focused on the airport.

That Trouble had acted by instinct never occurred to them. That he had slipped into the airport as an individual without an adult chaperone never occurred to them. That he had acted alone was unthinkable.

And even if they had thought of such things it would not have mattered. They needed the boy. It would be good if he were alive, but dead would be Plan B. That would be after Plan A managed to get him to tell where the box of precious stones was and whatever else he might know about things that had been discovered in Taj's flat and perhaps shared with others.

SIXTEEN

Preacherman and Trouble understood their predicament. They understood that the path to the future required them to resolve the issues. They had done no one wrong. They had been done wrong. The battle had been brought to them. But something was wrong . . . very wrong . . . and they were caught in the crosshairs.

Trouble did not know any of his relatives, who they were, or where they lived. He lived for the hope of one day finding family, especially his dad.

He had never had a childhood. He did not have a close friend. The only person inside his private world since the death of his mother was Preacherman. He trusted Preacherman.

They had each saved the other's life.

Preacherman had no known kin. He had taken a liking to Trouble. Their worlds had collided together like a big bang. The boy was smart and had grit. He was fearless. He had never known a non-Navajo to be accepted as an equal. His life had been saved by Trouble in the attack by the mountain lion. He had a debt to pay. He would protect the boy.

SEVENTEEN

Morning came on the reservation. It was not a normal morning like back in the city. No phones or recording devices where discussions were being held about selling the stones.

A Navajo chef from Chicago had arrived overnight, along with a body-builder from Los Angeles. Their assignment was to put pounds on Trouble, as pounds of muscle, not fat. In addition to gaining weight, he would be improving his Navajo language skills.

The chef's job was to prepare healthy meals. And there was another task for the chef. He was to include herbal supplements—part of ancient Indian medicine that would deepen the pigment of skin, a toning that would be temporary. The deeper tan would help to prevent sunburn.

Trouble was not an outsider. He came to breakfast in breechcloth and with the claw of the mountain lion he had killed hanging on a piece of leather around his neck.

He knew the plan and that his part of the plan was critical. He was ready for action.

EIGHTEEN

Officer Ramírez reentered his home with a sense of anxiety. If a car had been waiting for Preacherman and Trouble, then it was possible that he and his wife would be suspected.

Who was in the car that followed the taxi? Was it police officers or federal agents? Or was it bad men trying to find Trouble?

Whoever it was, they would logically extend their search to the Ramírez home. He and his wife could be in danger. Even if police only interrogated them, it could mean danger for Preacherman and Trouble. He was glad he had given Preacherman and Trouble a means of contacting him.

He and his wife talked and packed. About 4 a.m., they eased their car out the gated entrance and headed toward the Adirondack Mountains. A friend had a vacation cottage always open to the Ramírez couple. He knew the code to the lock and that it was vacant for a few weeks.

Before time to be in the office, Ramírez called his commander to share that a family emergency had occurred and he would need to take leave time. Later in the day, his commander reflected that two weeks would be past the time of Officer Ramírez's being able to retire with 30 years of service. The commander talked with the chief. They agreed that Ramírez would probably not return to duty. A ceremony would be planned for a later time.

A call from Ramírez did not come, but papers did—papers filing for retirement and indicating that he would not be able to attend a ceremony. He would have all items belonging to the department delivered by FedEx.

NINETEEN

Jeb knew that using any official government channels to try to find the boy would be a violation of protocol. He would have to depend on personal meetings with trusted friends and confidants. He did have the advantage of access to police reports about the bombing in the airport with video analysis of the boy throwing the backpack.

In off-duty hours, Jeb began to study crime in the area of the city where Trouble had most often been seen. It was like putting a thousand-piece puzzle together with only muted and blended colors—no one piece was distinctive. Over time, Jeb took notice that Officer Ramírez seemed to become a hero at solving crimes which too often included black cars, lots of violence, explosions, and dead people.

Jeb began to wonder if Trouble was a constant in the various episodes. Added to the history was the nasty explosion of the black car on the boulevard. It had taken investigators some time to figure out the parts made up four bodies. And like so many other crime scenes, the car had illegal plates with false registration.

Forensics had a nightmare with the body parts that could be found. No ID of any of the passengers, only a determination they would have been of Asian descent.

Jeb came across references to a Navajo Indian who might have been associated with the boy. But he could not find any hard evidence of relationship or their presence together in public places. No records. Who was the Navajo? What was his history?

Jeb asked a favor of a colleague in the FBI. A picture of the Navajo with name came through. He ran the name through the Veteran's Administration records.

The military history of the Navajo was impeccably clean: No violations; honor after honor; medal after medal for heroism; cited as "brillant," "fearless," "a true warrior," "night scout," and "the best of the best of special forces." The Navajo had carried out classified missions that would never be made public.

Jeb was beginning to think he had a lead. But there were many questions to which he did not have answers. Who was the boy? Where did he come from? Where did he live? Why were there no public records of the boy? Who were his parents or guardians? How could he just disappear from the airport?

His mind kept coming back to Officer Ramírez. He decided to pay a quiet visit to the home of the officer. When he arrived, he found an empty house with a "For Sale" sign. When he called the phone number on the sign, it was an attorney's office.

The attorney declined to answer any questions, only revealing that he was authorized to sell the property for his client.

TWENTY

In the penthouse, all hell was breaking loose. The precious stones were missing. The explosion where the Navajo had lived had not left a single item worth putting in a flea market. The still smoking ruins were cordoned off as a possible crime scene and under 24-hour police surveillance. A car had been bombed and four of their best hit men were dead.

On the other side of the world, meetings were in process questioning those in charge of cartel business in the United States. Heads were going to roll. A complex and long-term international smuggling operation was at risk.

Where had the Navajo and the boy gone? How could they have disappeared? How could they vanish without the police having a trace? They had enough operatives inside law enforcement to know that no evidence of bodies had been found in the burned ruins.

How many dead bodies and lost vehicles before investigators found clues pointing back to cartel operations? Were Feds already picking up enough information to be dangerous to cartel business? Were they running out of luck?

Where was the box with precious stones? What would happen if the box was not found? Anxiety was trending to fear.

What did the boy know about the computers in the basement of the flat? Who was the Old Man that kept getting in the way of their finding the boy?

There were too many things going wrong. They had questions. They did not have answers. They were angry.

Fear is powerful. Fear in the heart of evil people is reckless and brutal. If they lose, they lose everything. Restraint is not an option. Violence is preferred to failure.

What they had to lose was an international network that had been developed over decades and involved high-level officials in numerous nations. Their fortunes and lives were at risk.

TWENTY-ONE

Azian's dream of owning and piloting a Gulfstream had come true. His copilot was attentive, but relaxed. High over the Atlantic at 600 mph a tailwind was pushing ground speed of almost 700 mph. His adrenalin would have been pumping with excitement, except that he was constantly thinking about Rahel's son. While at the controls, his mind was thinking about a boy.

He would have lunch with Stewart and Alaina in the evening. They would share information and discuss possibilities surrounding the search for the boy.

He felt hope in knowing the boy could be alive. And it was gratifying to have others to talk to and help.

As he feathered a landing of the Gulfstream, he subconsciously reflected that his father was a formidable opponent. If only he knew what was in his father's heart and mind.

Walking into the private plane section of the terminal, he felt the weight of his dufflebag to be light compared to the weight on his heart. His dad had many good qualities, yet the shadow of his dad's lust for power and wealth pushed away any hope for a happy ending.

He was confident that Kahlil's investigators were searching for Rahel and a child. It occurred to him that his father probably did not know that Rahel was dead.

A cold shudder passed over him as he thought about some of the men who had done work for his father in the past. Were they still obligated to his father? Were they still employed by him?

Azian did not know. He hoped not.

TWENTY-TWO

Syed was sailing around East Timor when a distress signal was received. A pirate attack was in process.

His ship was by far closest to the ship sending the distress signal.

Going to the command center, he relieved the first mate. His crew did not know that he had made an overnight venture with Israeli specialists to test the ship and its weapons. But this was Syed's first time to command the ship in a possible battle. His men were not warriors. They had never been in a violent confrontation with another ship.

The crew was aware of a few rifles and pistols on the ship. Such weapons were secured in Captain Syed's quarters.

Syed instructed them to secure objects on deck and prepare for maximum speed. The off-duty crew members were to go to their private quarters.

Syed made a slight change of course and then gave a command to the engine room for max speed. Even his engineers did not know what they were about to experience.

As Syed pressed a button, ballasts on sides of the ship filled with air. The powerful engines torched as the ship seemed to lift out of the water. It was an exhilarating feeling— almost like being airborne.

A smaller vessel well-armed was attacking a large yacht. The sounds of gunfire could be heard as they approached and smoke was rising from the deck of the yacht being attacked. The pirate boat assumed that the approaching ship was not armed. The assumption was a terrible mistake.

Captain Syed pressed a button and a steel shutter retracted. A laser gun moved on tracks and radar focused on the rear of the pirate boat. A blast from the laser gun disabled the motor.

Then a canister ejected above the pirate boat, as Captain Syed pressed another button. Smoke smothered the pirate boat. Syed locked the pirate boat on radar and rolled out a Japanese APHE. After 400 bullets in barely 30 seconds, Syed paused the APHE.

Slowing his ship, he waited for the smoke to clear. There appeared to be no one moving on the pirate boat. It would sink, even though Syed had tried to put most of the bullets along the top of the deck.

He made a decision to board and investigate. Only one person was found alive, barely alive. One of Captain Syed's crew spoke the language and was able to get him to talk. They were pirates who had recently sunk another ship and left no survivors.

Crewmen swung a crane from Syed's ship and worked frantically to salvage cargo, not knowing contents. Most cargo was saved. They watched the pirate boat sink with a few boxes of freight still on the deck.

The last pirate died talking about being part of something big as the whole world. It was strange talk he muttered in his last moments. The boat was abandoned to Davy Jones' Locker with bodies of the pirates on board.

Captain Syed approached the yacht that had been attacked. It was a fancy 65-footer being delivered to a sheik. Bullets from the pirate boat had damaged the yacht, disabling its engine. Fortunately, the vessel was seaworthy. Probably, the pirates had exercised restraint, in hopes of making the yacht their new home.

The nearest port was about 30 nautical miles. Captain Syed instructed his crew to attach tow lines to the yacht. It was the right thing to do. Honor on the high seas is without nationality.

The powerful engines were not strained, but the speed was slowed. The pirate incident was reported to the port authority.

What Captain Syed did not know was that the captain of the yacht had sent a message to the owner who was an Arab sheik. When they pulled into port, authorities took Captain Syed to a phone.

The sheik called to express gratitude for Captain Syed's rescue of his daughter who had been on the yacht. He asked how he could arrange compensation for the rescue and towing.

Captain Syed declined the gift. The sheik insisted they meet. Captain Syed indicated he was heading to Australia. The sheik said he would travel to Sydney and meet Syed.

Captain Syed left the harbor and took notice that his crew was particularly upbeat. At first he thought it was his imagination, but the change in his crew was unmistakable. They were polishing handrails and scrubbing decks. He wondered if his imagination was exaggerating. Did he sense a new enthusiasm?

He smiled to himself. The ship had performed excellently. His men were now aware that there were secrets of the ship making it special. Their pride to serve on the ship had increased.

He decided that maybe retiring would be pushed back a little more. What could be more exciting than being on his ship on the high seas? Besides, there was the boy. He would not rest until he knew the boy was well. Davy Jones would just have to be patient.

Later that evening they opened the cargo boxes from the pirate ship. While much of the contraband was common goods, they also found jewelry, watches, necklaces, rings and thousands of dollars in coins and bills from different countries. Three crates of Russian AK47s and plenty of ammunition were secured in the captain's quarters.

Syed decided the money would be equally divided among crew members. They were ecstatic.

But wisely he shared that distribution would not happen until a time when they would be given extended shore leave.

It could have been easily disregarded and discarded, but a small leather satchel was pulled out of a duffel bag. Crew members were too engaged with talk about the money and guns to notice that Captain Syed deftly slipped the satchel inside his uniform.

That evening in the privacy of his quarters, Syed began a study of the papers. There were references about contacts in different countries. Most of the papers were in a language not familiar to Syed.

He came to the conclusion that the papers had been taken by the pirates from another ship. Perhaps, the pirates had not been able to read or understand the papers. Maybe they had not even opened the package. Maybe they were to deliver the papers to another contact.

The papers were placed in the safe in his quarters. They would need translation and careful study.

He would see Stewart in New York City. Together they would find a translator.

But first he must stop in Australia.

TWENTY-THREE

Officer Ramírez followed the news about happenings back in the city. He took note that no mention was made of bodies being recovered. Also no evidence had been salvaged from the ruins identifying previous occupants. Ramírez assumed that Preacherman and Trouble were still alive.

There were pictures of the boy, but no data was publicly shared that would have linked the boy to Preacherman or Officer Ramírez.

A few days later, Ramírez arranged to borrow a motorhome from a friend. His friend met him, and they exchanged vehicles. Ramírez made his car a gift to his friend so the title could be changed.

He had promised his wife that one day they would adventure. It was time to live their dream of touring the United States. His police experience was helpful. They would use cash. By not staying in motels and using cash it would be hard to be traced or followed.

A Russian pistol, rifle with a scope, and plenty of ammunition were hidden under linens in a drawer.

They took caution not to sign anything as they traveled. They never planned tomorrow until after breakfast. They took country roads. Sometimes, they took dead-end roads to see if anyone was following them. He had been a policeman long enough to know that the best of secrets can leak.

The one constant was that every day Ramírez's wife talked about the boy. Most of the time she talked, and he listened. The boy had touched a nerve deep within her. She was taking on a new energy. Her voice seemed pitched a little higher and with new energy.

Ramírez wondered how many hours he would have to listen to his wife talk about the boy. She never used the name "Trouble." She would say, "The boy" with a gentleness that he could not explain. She had come to care about the boy in a way that seemed to fit her empty mother's heart. It was sacred territory. It was better for him to be silent.

While he listened, he was doing a lot of thinking. Could it be that their paths would cross again with the Navajo and the boy?

He had not been to church for many years. As he turned in for the night he breathed a prayer asking God to watch over Trouble and Preacherman. He paused and then added, "I promise to be better."

He and his wife had a hard time sleeping that night. They talked. They concocted scenarios of what could be. They imagined, dreamed, and woke to a new day as if they were 20 years younger.

Later that morning, Ramírez checked a phone Preacherman had given him. Other Tuesdays had passed with no message. This morning there was a message leaving a phone number he was to call.

He stopped at a Walmart to purchase a burner phone. His hands were trembling when he dialed the number. It was a recorded message.

The message was short and to the point. "We are well . . . will be in touch soon."

That was all. No more. He called three different times to listen to the same message, hoping for more; but there was no more.

He never knew how many times his wife called to listen to the message.

Weeks passed. Ramírez and his wife were sitting quietly by a two-sided fire pit in a Colorado park. A camper backed into the space next to them. Such was normal on travel campgrounds.

The driver of the other vehicle casually set up camp and built his fire on the other side of Ramírez's pit. Courtesies were exchanged. They chatted about the leaves turning color, fish jumping in the stream, and the feeling of fall in the air.

Next morning the other camper was gone. They had not heard the departure. When Ramírez was packing up, he opened a toolbox door to find a cell phone with a note to call Preacherman, and then throw the phone into the river.

Though he was tempted to call immediately, he sensed that it would be wise to have his wife present for the call. Going back into the camper, he showed her the note. They closed all windows, sat down together and dialed the number.

It was a recorded message. "Officer Ramírez, our men have been following you since you left home. Would you and your wife be interested in living in our new home? It will be in the suburbs of New York City. Think it over. You will be contacted in a few days. Know we are near at all times. It was one of our men who left this phone."

Ramírez and his wife talked. She asked: "Why wait? Why wait a few days? Can we not give the answer now?"

He knew the answer they would give. There was a gentleness of a smile that was slipping across her face with a glow, making her look years younger.

Then she was in his lap, kissing him—passionately—giggling, laughing, running her fingers through his hair, and telling him how much she loved him.

He wondered if he had spent too many hours and years doing police work. He should have stayed home more.

They decided to stay in the camp another day.

TWENTY-FOUR

Preacherman was spending long hours with runners who were going and coming all over the world. He knew the runners would die before giving information leading back to the reservation or sharing details of the operation.

Contacts had been developed in various countries. A system for transporting the precious stones was carefully strategized. It would take about a month for cash to begin to flow into a Swedish bank account.

A nonprofit foundation had been established to receive the funds designated for the Navajo infrastructure project. Corruption was too easy. The money would be secured to projects with careful supervision of employed professionals who were trustworthy and loyal. It would be a nongovernmental operation with only a small fee to pacify reservation bureaucracy.

The agreement had been carefully written that if Navajo tribal officials refused to cooperate, funds could be used for other native reservations that would be happy to cooperate.

Trouble's daily regimen began before daylight and ended at sundown, except when there were night ventures. Occasionally, a half-day of reprieve was allowed. The leaders had all served in Special Forces and maintained their physical regimen. Diet was carefully regulated. Exercise programs included mountain climbing, desert walks, carrying heavy loads, and swimming. There was zero tolerance for alcohol, tobacco, or drugs.

Trouble lost three pounds. Then slowly his muscles began to tighten, his biceps changed, and his chest took on muscle.

In the third week of training, Indian wrestling was introduced. He watched. Then it was his turn to enter the ring. He wondered the following morning if every bone in his body were broken. How could you hurt so bad and still be alive?

Breakfast was served. He soon found himself jogging down a trail with aching muscles screaming. But as the morning progressed, the pain eased. When they came to a mountain stream, he swam. It was soothing.

His body was toning. The olive hue of his skin was giving way to a bronze hue.

Runners were connecting with buyers. Some $4 million had been deposited into the Swiss account. The process was working smoothly.

While it's a big world, when millions of dollars in unregistered and uncut precious stones hit the black market, there is an underground pipeline. Talk was happening. And the talk was making its way to cartel leaders. The fingers of the underworld are long and tenacious, greedy, and relentless, persistent, and brutal.

Fortunately for Preacherman and Trouble, no clue was being left that would allow others to trace transactions back to the reservation.

However in Vienna, Austria, a runner had been followed for days. It was morning. He entered a Swiss bank and made a deposit of $2 million, bringing the total to $12,800,000 in that account. He was dressed immaculately and expensively. When depositing large sums, it is wise to look in character.

He knew that he had been followed. Pausing before exiting, he placed the well-worn Louis Vuitton leather case under his left arm leaving his right arm free.

Exiting the bank, he turned toward a canal instead of returning to his car. About a block from the bank, three men rushed toward him as he rounded a corner. In a deft move, he turned his body allowing the ends of the briefcase to point toward two of the men and pressed the remote control. A brace of pistols inside the briefcase fired, neutralizing two victims.

The Navajo's right arm was already extended with a ten-inch double-bladed knife that had ejected from his coat sleeve. The third man would not talk again, even if he lived.

The runner knew there were other men who had been near his car. Sprinting 20 yards, he fastened the briefcase to his body and dove into the canal. By the time he came up on the other side of a boat, he was in swimming trunks and carrying the briefcase.

Over the next few days, messages kept coming back to Preacherman and all the runners that greater caution would need to be exercised.

TWENTY-FIVE

Ten, twelve, fourteen pounds—Trouble's body was taking on muscle.

The Indian wrestling was a discipline of the mind—never think defeat.

As if the wrestling were not challenging enough, Trouble was not at all excited with what happened one evening after they had eaten. They were sitting around a campfire when a cage was set down in the middle of their circle. A rattlesnake was allowed to exit through a trap door.

One of the warriors taunted the snake until it was coiled with rattlers singing an angry song. The Navajo continued to jab with a stick until the serpent struck.

What astonished Trouble was that the native caught the rattlesnake just behind its head.

One by one the natives took turns with the rattlesnakes. None of them were bitten. All of them caught the snake by its neck.

There was silence. Only one warrior remained. It was Trouble's turn. He remembered being frightened in the flat when bad men had captured him. He remembered a few other times of close calls or accidents. But the idea of being bitten by a rattlesnake was a fear he had not known.

He had no choice. He tried. It did not work. The rattlesnake bit him. He just stood there wondering how long he would live, but thinking he should have already been dead in past experiences.

For the first time, he heard Indians laugh.

Then one of them shared that the snakes had all been defanged. They had no poison; he would live.

After the laughter settled, another rattler crawled out. It was much larger. Trouble experienced several more bites before successfully grabbing one just behind its head.

Stone-faced Navajos sat quietly. They did not applaud. They did not show emotion. One by one they rose and drifted into the night.

Navajos know when a boy becomes a man. A brave is not applauded.

TWENTY-SIX

Azian, Stewart, and Alaina found a private corner table on the patio of a restaurant at the harbor. Their conversation lasted for hours as they exchanged information and developed plans.

Alaina made arrangements for Azian to meet Jeb. They were hopeful that Azian could share information with Jeb that might assist in Jeb's efforts to find the boy.

Azian left. He wanted a good night's rest. Tomorrow he would travel for his meeting with Jeb.

TWENTY-SEVEN

Stewart wanted to retrace some of Captain Syed's story by visiting places where Rahel had been. While the flat no longer existed, he wanted to drive by the location. He asked Alaina to go with him. From the area of the flat, they traveled to the pauper's cemetery—such a place as Stewart had not known even existed.

His emotions were a wreck. The battle inside him was raging like a fever.

To think of Rahel's dying alone and being buried without a name was humiliating. To think she had been willing to suffer such loneliness and pain to protect him and their son was unfathomable. What kind of fear could have driven her to such extremes? He wondered what things he did not know about her culture.

Alaina was silent for a long while, but finally she spoke.

"Stewart, did you have to have a blood test for a marriage license?"

"Yes," he said softly.

"Why not have DNA pulled from the marriage blood sample and petition the City of New York to exhume the body and test the DNA? If it is Rahel's body, you can have her body moved to your family cemetery in England."

Stewart was thinking, hesitating.

Alaina continued. "If it is Rahel's DNA, you may need the evidence to prove the identity of your son. The photograph shown you by Captain Syed is several years old. He will have changed, and you may need proof of kinship."

Stewart made a phone call to corporate attorneys to arrange for Rahel's body to be exhumed for a DNA test.

They drove toward the elementary school where Trouble had attended. At the school, Stewart and Alaina met the man who had replaced the lady principal. It was the charm of Alaina that persuaded the principal to share Trouble's school record. However, the principal would not give them any printed records to keep.

When the file was placed in front of them, Stewart gasped. The name Sir Walter Scott was beside the photo of the boy.

Alaina could tell that Stewart was shaken and thoughtfully decided silence would bring an answer.

Stewart finally spoke, though his voice was barely audible: "That is the title of her book that I picked up off the walk the first time we met!"

He did not tell her that Rahel had given him the same book on their wedding day. Inside the cover she had written: "To My Only Love who walked with me in the rain, and made time stand still."

Silently, they continued to read the notes: No discipline problem; periodic absences without excuses; superb scores; respectful; never shared about family, except to say his mother was ill, and a reference that he believed his father was alive—though no name was given for a father.

No record of his mother having come to school with him since the first day of his enrollment in second grade. He was not anti-social, but he did not develop intense friendships. He had insisted his name was Sir Walter Scott. Students had called him "Walter." Because of gifts he gave other students, they thought he was rich, though mysterious.

There were notes of visits to the home. No one had been allowed beyond the front door. When the boy began to miss more school, no one answered the door of the flat when social workers visited.

The DNA test was already in process, but after seeing the school records, Stewart needed no further evidence. Like troubled waters calm after a storm, Stewart knew that he had a son. This was the first physical evidence that his son might be alive. The challenge was to find his son—if he was still alive.

The final note in the school records was a recommendation for the school social worker to investigate. However, Trouble never returned to school and the flat was demolished. There was no forwarding address for the boy.

Stewart and Alaina walked out of the principal's office, down the sidewalk, and kept walking. Not a word was spoken.

Alaina discreetly observed Stewart's jaw muscles contracting. His cheeks were flushed with a touch of red. His eyes were moist. Several times she noticed that he would draw his fingers into a tight fist and then seem to relax.

It would be better to let him speak first. She was in his world. His emotions were traveling at high speed trying to reconcile broken pieces.

His pace had quickened until she was struggling to keep up. She knew that he was unaware of her effort to keep pace. Fortunately for her, he turned suddenly and sat down on a bench at a table in a park. She silently took a seat on the other side of the table.

He was morphing as she watched the change in his expression. His jaw was set in resolve. His pupils narrowed in focus.

He looked at her and began to apologize, "Oh, Alaina, I am so sorry. I did not realize I was taxing you so with my fast walk. Forgive me. These years have been an inordinate grief to my heart, not knowing where Rahel could be. Not having any idea whether she were alive, in need, or safe, not knowing whether she gave birth, and if so whether the child lived and was a boy or girl."

"Seeing the boy in the airport . . . talking to Syed . . . meeting Azian . . . learning of Rahel's death . . . visiting her grave . . . realizing that I have a son, alive and in danger . . . my mind and emotions are in deep conflict."

Alaina held her silence.

Stewart charged on. "For the first time in my life, I am angry. It is a burning anger. Rahel, I cannot help. But I have a son. I will find him at all costs! I will find him! God help me if I encounter those who would harm him."

Alaina's eyes were moist with tears as she whispered, "Stewart, I will help . . . I too will help."

They talked long. They talked about how quickly events had changed their lives. They talked about their first meeting in Calgary. He laughed as if embarrassed when she reminded him that he left Canada abruptly.

They took hope that Captain Syed would be a helpful partner in the search. There was disappointment that Jeb had not been able to learn more from his contacts with federal authorities.

Stewart and Alaina had not spent a night together. They had not even kissed. Alaina had sensed he needed time. He was a gentleman. Honor was above all. Love is not to be awakened before its time.

They rose to leave, walking through a flower garden. Children were playing at a birthday party. The air was gentle. Soft guitar music could be heard from someone who loved music and the outdoors.

There was no certain moment that precipitated the move. It was like an unconscious happening. Stewart slipped his hand into Alaina's. Not a word was spoken. They walked on as if it was natural.

But in Alaina's heart, something happened. She knew what she had never known before. She could have waited a hundred years for this moment. Parents and relatives had puzzled why such a gorgeous and rich woman was still single. Many had attempted to put a ring on her finger.

Alaina was a romantic. She had set her heart to be single all her life—until . . .

Now she had other thoughts for the future.

TWENTY-EIGHT

Months passed. In the corner of the reservation, it was like a war camp with scouts going and coming. Security was totally intense.

The good news was that estimates of proceeds from sales of the precious stones had been low. The quality of the diamonds and other stones was finest grade. The fact that there was no legal or business record of them was positive. Final sales would exceed $50 million, if all connections were made. Preacherman assured the warriors that the 50/50 agreement would stand.

Preacherman was pleased with the change in Trouble's physique and the deepening tone of his skin. His wrestling skills were admired by the other Navajos.

Trouble was exposed to different types of weapons. What he did not put his hands on and use, he studied or listened to those who had used such weapons. If he could not operate them, at least he understood the principle, the function, and the power of the weapons.

The plan Preacherman and Trouble developed was working. It was time to move to the next level. They knew too much, had seen too much, and they had both been in times and places and witnessed crimes that made them prime targets. They were living with a bull's-eye on their backs.

They had a solution. The solution was not to wait. They would take the battle to the bad guys, whoever they were and wherever they were. They would choose the terms for justice.

TWENTY-NINE

Contact had been made with Ramírez. The officer and his wife had been followed by Navajos every day since they had left home. Preacherman was convinced they were good people who could be trusted.

He and Trouble would need friends. The warriors had done their job well. A few of them would be traveling with Preacherman and Trouble to New York City.

Others would be left to make sure that funds were disbursed and projects on the reservation kept honest. They would be needed on the reservation to ensure that corrupt people did not prevent thc proposed water projects. Too often on reservations, monies allocated by Congress for American Indians had failed to reach those in need. A lot of sticky fingers can make rich folks of a few and keep the majority still struggling in poverty.

It was time to change identities. Preacherman had served in Vietnam with a soldier who later developed superior skills in creating aliases with all the appropriate documentation. Arrangements were made to bring him to the reservation for meetings with Preacherman and Trouble.

Discussions were long and intense to develop a plausible history that would alter their identities and appearances. With photographs done and documents ready, it was time to test the process.

That night Preacherman and Trouble talked. They understood that off the reservation, they were wanted by good guys and bad guys. Practically every federal agency was involved in an effort to bring them in for questioning about the airport bombing and what appeared to be related events.

What they did not know was the FBI had concluded that there was a link between the Navajo, the boy, and the bad guys. The Feds believed the boy might have information about an international crime ring. Why were Preacherman and Trouble wanted by bad people in other countries? The plot was thickening, yet it was a plot-defying logic.

Trouble would stay on the reservation under watchful eyes and continue his regimen of diet, exercise, and training. The pounds he had gained were barely noticeable because of a growth spurt in height and muscle development.

He was learning the Navajo language and would continue to practice with different kinds of weapons. His skill with native weapons had come to be admired by other warriors. He was exceptionally accurate with the nonreturning boomerang developed by indigenous tribes of Australia.

Preacherman was leaving the reservation. He would be traveling for about a month. The plan would be to meet Trouble in New York.

Just before dawn, a limo eased out of bushes onto Route 66 heading east. Two hours later, a burnt orange sun was warming up the morning when Preacherman exited the vehicle in Gallup.

This was to be the litmus test. His beard was full, grey, and professionally trimmed. His hair was short and with a gentleman's cut. Colored contact lenses in his eyes, light touches of cosmetics, and a Loro Piana suit were intended to test the locals. Would he be recognized? Preacherman entered Earl's Restaurant. A gold-plated cane with intricate carvings and a ten-carat diamond ring added a distracting dash.

The cane was dazzling in appearance. Inside the delicate art was a seven-shot .38 caliber with hollow-bore bullets.

As a boy, Preacherman had been to the restaurant countless times, even working as a dishwasher for about six months while in high school. Home on leave from the military and visiting the reservation, Earl's was always on his agenda. Food was terrific, and it was a place to meet friends and keep up with the culture and politics. He had not been to Earl's since Trouble had become a primary part of his life.

What he would not do was talk while in the restaurant. His voice would be telltale. A Navajo knows the voice of a Navajo. There is distinction of inflection that cannot be erased with time. Certain words have their watermark. His chauffeur was a Jamaican who would order for him, giving the illusion that he did not speak English or Navajo.

Earl's is a friendly diner. Outside during daylight hours, Navajos display jewelry, pottery, and other native-made items, hoping to attract tourist dollars. A few vendors go from table to table inside the restaurant. The owner may stop by a table and chat. Walls are decorated with native art. A picture of Night Stalker in uniform was hanging on the wall near the cash register.

About halfway through the meal, a woman holding an exquisite Navajo wedding pitcher approached the table. Preacherman knew her from high school. He kept his face slightly down and continued to eat. His chauffeur listened to the woman trying to sell her autographed crafts.

She kept glancing toward Preacherman as if puzzled, but then seemed to relax as the Jamaican handed her a $100 bill for the pottery, which included a generous tip. She moved on and did not look back. Preacherman believed that she had not recognized him.

Meal finished, there was quite a buzz as Preacherman made his exit with the chauffeur going before him and opening the limo door. People inside and outside were fixated on the ostentatious display of wealth.

Traveling I-40 east, they left the reservation. Albuquerque Airport is off the Navajo Nation reservation, but it is distinctly associated with Indian culture. Colors and designs approaching the airport testify to the heritage of native America. Inside the airport, rugs and crafts made by American Indians are displayed as museum pieces or listed for sale.

The city of Albuquerque acts as a gateway to the world of native Indians where time still seems to stand still. It is like a line of demarcation between the worlds of the white man and the red man.

Numerous employees are native Indians, and there are always Indians traveling to and from the two different worlds.

It seemed prudent for Preacherman to avoid Albuquerque and depart from Las Vegas. Rich folks were the norm in the casino capitol of the West. Splashing wealth was the culture. One more rich man would not disturb the equilibrium of a city taking pride in whatever pleasures and thrills money can buy.

Preacherman had no intention of leaving any money in Las Vegas. His intent was a quiet and quick exit from the United States.

At the airport, Preacherman tipped the chauffeur and was soon seated first class to Australia. There would be two changes of planes before he reached his destination.

He marked the menu request and decided that silence would best serve him for the duration of the trip.

Sydney was a new adventure for Preacherman. He decided to stay in the urban area two or three days to adjust to the culture and learn from natives and locals about gold mining in Australia.

Much homework had been done before his arrival. He had already purchased an old gold mine that had been closed for decades. When he arrived at the mine, he wanted to talk the language and convince the manager of the mine that accountability would be expected. Research had indicated new types of engineering could make the mine profitable.

The gold mine had been purchased to serve as a mechanism for moving funds. The intent was not to lose money. Ownership of the mine was part of the validation of his and Trouble's new aliases.

New technology was more efficient than when the mine had been closed decades ago. The gold was higher grade and greater yield than anticipated. The mine would be profitable.

Additional minerals were byproducts of the gold mining. New equipment was ordered. Arrangements would need to be made for bulk shipping of the byproducts from mining gold.

Back in Sydney, Preacherman explored which shipping company was considered honest and reliable. He was referred to a branch office of a corporation with headquarters in England.

On his way to the airport, he decided to stop by and talk with executives of the shipping company. In the entrance foyer, a portrait of the CEO arrested Preacherman. While he could not put his finger on any one thing about the features of the man in the picture there was a hint of familiarity that left him restless. He could not resolve what it was about the picture that gave him a feeling he knew the person.

The CEO was away on a trip. Preacherman left Information for the CEO to contact him.

In leaving the executive offices, Preacherman paused in the lobby to study the portrait again. He came to no conclusion other than the man in the portrait reminded him of someone he had met or that he knew.

He landed at Kennedy Airport with the puzzle of the portrait tucked away in his subconscious as an open agenda.

THIRTY

The last transaction of the precious stones was expected to be a quiet delivery to New York City. It was the only sale that had been made inside the United States. Two warriors were selected for the contact, but with a backup plan. There had been no incident since Vienna, but there had been several close calls. Great caution was being exercised to prevent compromising the total operation.

At the last minute, the Navajos altered location to a park on Long Island where a seller was to meet a purchaser. It was an open area of about an acre. The only other persons in the park were preparing for a hot-air balloon takeoff, which was why the Navajos chose the setting. One of the Navajos meandered casually toward the balloon. He spoke with the people in the balloon and gave them a roll of $100 bills, as prearranged.

The other Navajo, who appeared to be alone, moved toward a fountain area that had been agreed as the meeting point. A man was waiting. The transaction was effected efficiently and in a nonsuspicious manner.

Barely had items exchanged hands when the purchaser reached into his pocket to extract a gun. He never knew when a dart coated with drugs penetrated his body, stunning him with the impact, and in seconds leaving him immobile.

The Navajo who had received the money ran to the hot-air balloon and jumped in just as it was rising off the ground.

Six men came out of bushes running toward the man who had been immobilized by the dart. With the balloon rising above the treetops and policemen coming from all directions, the six men made a quick decision to hide their guns and run to a nearby car. The car left with tires squealing.

Policemen on bicycles converged to the place where the man lay beside a leather satchel with uncut and unregistered stones. Once again, the police found no clue pointing them to Preacherman or Trouble.

There would be unhappy people in many places with the loss of the money and the stones. Anger would turn to fury when they concluded that a Navajo and a street boy had outwitted them.

Two miles north, both the Navajos parachuted from the balloon leaving it to sail on. Their target landing was a farm field where a rental car was parked under a bridge.

They quickly gathered their parachutes into clumps. Changing clothes, they put everything they took off in bags with the parachutes. A container of acid was removed from the car and poured over parachutes and clothes. In a couple of hours, the acid would leave nothing that would serve forensics.

Driving carefully they made their way to Route 87, called "Northway." The goal was to be in Albany before sunset.

Following the Hudson River, they eased northward through Sarasota Springs to Pottersville—a very mountainous area with no cell phone service. They were on their own.

Fortunately, they had been warned that Glens Falls, NY can be a speed trap. How else does a remote community get money from folks passing through? They also knew that getting stopped could lead to more questions than they wanted to answer. Navajos do not tend to wander around in sacred land of the Mohicans.

Between Great Falls and Warrensburg, they turned unto a logging trail for a couple of miles. Wiping down the car carefully, they left the keys in the gas flap.

Later, an anonymous call would report the location of the car.

Just before dawn, they were in the helicopter that had been left for them. It did not take long to land on the shore of Lake Champlain.

They hastened to a Hustler 41 Razor sitting in nearby waters and tied to a tree. Time was of the essence as they made their way southwest into Lake Michigan.

Slowing the engine to reduce wake, they came alongside a small boat. Occupants changed boats.

Without a word exchanged, the Navajo who had brought the smaller boat took the Hustler and left. He knew what to do.

The two warriors with the money and survival supplies slowly made their way toward shore. After removing the money and supplies, one of the Navajos put a hole in the bottom of the boat, pointed it out into deep waters and taped the switch of the engine. The boat would sink a few miles from shore.

They would be off the grid with nature and God for a couple of weeks. Camping out and protecting $6 million cash. Others knew when to come for them. They knew when others would come. All was well.

THIRTY-ONE

The Feds had been carefully piecing together bits of information. One of the transactions for selling the diamonds had been done with an emissary of an Arab prince in Dubai. The FBI had managed to insert a tracking device in the Navajo's satchel while in an airport. The signal went dead on the Navajo reservation.

Since Feds dealing with crime on the Navajo Nation are sensitive, normally the FBI worked with Navajo police officials. However, a decision was made that the area to be explored was sufficiently remote to likely prevent the Navajos knowing about a raid. They decided to do the raid without contacting reservation authorities.

Satellite images had revealed human activity in an area basically uninhabited.

Four helicopters landed about dawn in the area where the last ping had been received from the tracking device in the Navajo's case. Each helicopter carried a SWAT team. Their information suggested that Navajos were connected to the sale of precious stones. They did not know if the Navajos were the good guys or the bad guys. They were prepared for the worst.

Fortunately for the Feds, they landed on a plateau. Just as the helicopters touched down, there were massive explosions in the valley below. Agents jumped from the choppers and took up battle positions. Their weapons were useless. There was no enemy to be seen. The dust from the explosion created zero visibility.

When the dust settled, there was nothing but barrenness. No sign of human life other than FBI SWAT members with camouflage uniforms looking dusty brown.

Diligently, they looked for human activity or evidence of a crime. Neither was to be found.

Command headquarters back in Phoenix was watching by video cam in real time. The order came to evacuate. Reservation police would be coming to investigate the explosion. The choppers took to canyons staying below radar.

Only one man among the FBI agents understood what had happened. His father was a Navajo who had left the reservation to attend Arizona State University and study criminology. He had met and married a Caucasian woman from Oregon and become a federal agent.

Their son had spent several summers during his youth on the reservation to qualify as a brave. The son had chosen to follow his dad and become a federal agent.

All the above was in the file of the agent on the chopper. His Navajo heritage was part of the reason he had been brought on the mission. He knew the language.

But the agent had not known there would be explosions. He was thankful that no damage had been done to federal equipment and there were no injuries. However, there was a lot of damage to pride.

He knew the resourcefulness of Navajos. If the other agents had looked closely, they would have detected laughter in his eyes.

To the Navajo, "The Long Walk" was yesterday. The memory of what their ancestors had endured had not faded over the years.

What none of the agents knew was that when the dust settled, two huge cliffs had tumbled together to form a natural dam. Melting snow and the valley stream would provide a reservoir of drinking water. It was part of the bigger plan to serve hundreds of homes and encourage farming.

EPA would not get an application for this reservoir. It would be considered an act of God.

THIRTY-TWO

Sitting on a butte for hours at a time and concentrating helps every sense become super acute. Long before radar would have picked up the approaching choppers, the Navajos were in exit mode. The explosives had been in place for weeks.

Careful plans had been made to leave no evidence behind when the time came to vacate. Items not needed were thrown into pits that would be covered by debris of the explosion. It would take centuries for the earth to reveal secrets. Future archeologists would puzzle and reconstruct strange scenarios that would only be partial truth.

For more than a hundred years, Navajos had been digging tunnels. The maze of passageways was so intricate that if a stranger had wandered into it, they likely would have died of exhaustion or snakebite before finding an exit.

Trouble and a group of Navajo warriors had left the camp through a tunnel hours before the FBI arrived. They moved through the darkness with Trouble having to trust the guide in front of him.

Though safely away from the effects of the explosion, they had felt the tremors of the earth and knew what was happening. The explosives had been planted by veterans who had taken out bridges and strategic targets in war. They were munitions experts. The major effects of the blasts would be contained in about a square mile.

What fascinated Trouble was that at times they would exit a tunnel, cross a stretch of land, and enter a new tunnel. He lost all sense of direction and wondered if they were going in circles. At times, the tunnel was natural and only crevices between rocks. More than once, they crawled through small openings or had to lie on the ground and wriggle their bodies to the other side.

Other parts of the tunnels had been dug by hand. Occasionally, there were arches where rocks had been piled to prevent cave-ins.

Every brave carried water, food, and survival gear. The pace was brisk, with occasional pauses to rest. Not a word was spoken. Flashlights were used only in tunnels. The few times they encountered rattlesnakes, a knife left the hand of a Navajo with speed and accuracy either severing the head or pinning the coiling, writhing body of the serpent to the ground until its head and rattles were removed. The poison would be milked and saved for antidote and hunting. The rattlers were a trophy. Seconds later, they moved on as if nothing had happened.

When moonlight was adequate, they trotted. Trouble kept pace. No mercy was extended. Mercy was not asked. Mercy was not expected.

Trouble had to concentrate, and yet his mind rehearsed past events. He remembered the days of scavenging for food, his mother's sickness, having to say "Goodbye" to her knowing she was dying, living in the streets, and finding secret places to hide. He also remembered the time in the flat when he was almost kidnapped or killed, the head injury, waking up in Preacherman's house, becoming brave, encounters with Officer Ramírez, the airport explosion, the past weeks on the reservation without technology—only knowing time by moon, sun, or shadows. He did not know what day of the week it was.

It had been different in the city. Every day had its rhythm—machines, cars, and people going to work, leaving work, shopping, playing, romancing, going to church, and committing crimes in smog and fog. He had studied city life until he could tell what day of the week it was by what he saw. He knew the regular folks, what time of day they traveled and which direction. Saturdays were the busiest. Sundays were the quietest.

He wondered where Preacherman was.

He felt as if he were suspended in space looking down on a surreal adventure of a fictional character. How could an Asian/English boy be running with a bunch of Navajos in the middle of the night? If strangers were looking they would see a wiry, lithe and bronzed Navajo in breechcloth only different because he was shorter in stature. There was one distinction—the claw of a mountain lion hung on a leather strap around his neck, bouncing against his chest.

Birthdays meant little to him. What was there to celebrate other than being alive and having hope?

"Maybe I'm morphing to be a Navajo," he mused. Then it occurred to him that he was Navajo. He spoke Navajo.

He wondered what boys his age typically were doing in the city. He did not know about other cities. But he had seen boys his size in New York City. He had seen children going to movies, playing baseball in grassy parks and basketball on asphalt courts.

He did not envy them. He did not think of himself doing the things he saw children do. It was just curious to muse about people who were his size—whatever age he was.

He had chosen his life. It had not been forced upon him. He had reported his mother's death from a pay phone. He had not asked for help. He chose not to. He knew his world and was comfortable in it. Courts and social services were alien and the thought of being a dependent in the legal system was unfathomable.

As his feet pounded the earth, he was brought back to the reality of rugged terrain. They began a descent down a dangerous slope. No time to think about anything but staying alive. Every step was an inch from death. More than once, they extended a rope with knots and had to work together as they hung out in space with brutal rock waiting hundreds of feet below for hapless victims.

Only moonlight.

Each depended upon the other. No room for error. One death could mean the death of all.

Muscles ached, and blisters were the lessor part of bruised feet from stone scrapings and cuts.

The mountains were behind them. They would see Gallup, but they had an appointment elsewhere.

The old bomb of a truck was waiting. They climbed in and the truck rumbled along the Low Road toward Klagotoh.

The truck stopped in a covering of willow trees. They were out and gone in seconds. No trace of their presence was left.

Dawn would come soon.

They walked into a stream and followed the flow of the water into a cave. To Trouble's astonishment, they were in a large room with other braves. There was food and a fire for heat. No conversation.

Trouble ate and lay down on a rock ledge. He fell asleep dreaming of flying a big and fast airplane. It was a good dream.

THIRTY-THREE

There was silence in Kahlil's house. Silence can be deadly. It was as if there were a living ghost in his house. Maybe everyone was thinking about Rahel, but no one was talking.

Why was Azian looking more and more like a hero in the house? What did others know that he did not know? Servants had known how Kahlil had treated Rahel. Did they know details about Rahel that he did not know?

Were others sensing Azian might know something? Were they hopeful?

One thing sure: Azian's gentle nature was winsome. His grandfather had been that kind of personality. Strong as steel, yet with gentleness that treasured others and an easy manner that was magnetic in relationships.

Kahlil had lived by raw power. Those who did not fear him, admired his strength. He knew that much of his ability to control people had come from intelligence, prestige, and the power of money.

This was a new battleground. In his own home, there was a war. It was not a war with weapons he was accustomed to using. He knew how to financially destroy opponents, politically assassinate, and use spies to gather information to use against enemies or force them to yield to his dominance. His had been a world ruthless and without regret—winner take all.

But the war in his household was one of silence. Tasks were performed by servants. Family followed routine. Dinner was gatherings with shallow or surface conversation and impersonal. His own family seemed to avoid looking him in the eye.

His wife was dutiful, but words were few. There was an air of detachment. A distance between them that even his lavish gifts did not bridge. Times of physical togetherness, while gratifying, were without intimacy of heart.

Like layers of an onion being peeled to the core, Kahlil was increasingly struggling to understand this strange war. His pride would not allow him to consult. He had been the prime mover in his family and business circles. Where could he turn? Who would dare tell him anything? Who would speak a word of correction to him? What questions could he ask to open doors for others to tell him of things he did not know?

He had built walls that others could not tear down, boxing himself in. He had built walls he did not know how to tear down.

How could he open his heart to tell of his anger and treatment of Rahel? How could he dare to let others know that he was thinking of trying to find and eliminate Rahel's husband when she disappeared? His sources had not been able to find Rahel. He had decided to wait until his daughter was found. Then he would craft a plan.

Kahlil was a man caught in a vortex . . . spiraling. Emotions had never been high on his chart. He had moved by cold rationale. He was beginning to understand that deep inside him was a battle greater than the war in his own house.

His father had been a man of great principle and highly respected. He remembered his dad quoting poets and sharing maxims that were intended to shape honest character and build integrity.

Kahlil's personal business ventures had begun under the tutelage of his dad. After his father's death, Kahlil had edged little by little away from the principled life of his father. His brilliance, legal knowledge, and skills in trade had rapidly expanded the family empire. The path to wealth became a ruthless path that marginalized integrity.

When money becomes a god, talk of integrity is verbiage used to manipulate conversation. All Kahlil had left in his empty soul were haunting memories of principles that had served his father well, memories which he repressed to ensure he was in control of his world.

It was midnight. Kahlil was sitting in the darkness looking out the window. The moon was descending to make way for the sun to rise. Stars were losing their glimmer. He fell asleep in his recliner and dreamed of Rahel running through the house, laughing with Azian chasing her, and servants moving aside and smiling.

It was a good dream. He slept peacefully for the first time in a long time and did not awaken until almost noon.

THIRTY-FOUR

Jeb had learned from Secret Service briefings that the President was following the story of the airport bombing and the boy in the video. There was anxiety in federal circles about the failed Fed raid on the reservation. Navajo leaders were angry.

In addition, concerns about international involvement in the airport bombing had resulted in additional security measures for the President's family.

It was the scuttlebutt talk where Jeb learned more of the nuances. Agents of other government organizations let little bits of information drop in their conversations over meals, in bars, and at social gatherings.

Federal agents often settle their families in communities that include other agents. The nature of their work raises concerns for the safety of their spouses and children, especially when they are on missions.

With no violation of law, careful ears can pick up a lot of information at a barbecue, social event, or funeral.

The story of the raid on the Navajo Nation had gone viral. While public media did not know details or share the story, many agents had been able to piece together the storyline of what had happened on the reservation.

There had been news stories about the new dam on the Navajo Nation having promise to serve hundreds of families with water. Conspiracy theorists were lighting up social media with explanations pointing fingers at the Feds.

Wherever the story of the raid was told among agents, there were lots of chuckles about the embarrassment of the

FBI. They had grossly underestimated the warrior mind of the Navajo.

More than once an old-timer among the group would tell a war story about the Navajo soldier who seemed to be primary in a lot of what was happening.

But try as he might, Jeb could not get any information that would be helpful for Alaina and Stewart to find the boy.

THIRTY-FIVE

Ramírez and his wife packed up and left the campground to meander their way toward New York. As they had done so many times before, they chose the sightseeing route instead of the Interstate.

Late morning, they were enjoying the ride, talking, and laughing as they traveled a rural road through an Indian reservation. It had been some time since they had seen another vehicle.

A loud explosion immediately was followed by the right front of the camper dropping to the road and lurching toward a ravine. Ramírez fought for control and brought the vehicle to a stop just shy of going over the precipice.

Ramírez knew a tire had blown. What he saw when he looked at the tire alarmed him. It had been neatly cut between treads making certain that a blow-out would happen.

Police officer instinct kicked in. The cut was a clean straight line that had etched into the fiber. If it had been road debris, the cut would have been jagged. Injury or death had been intended.

The tire was a secondary concern. They were in danger.

Ramírez retrieved the rifle and spoke calmly to his wife. At that moment, he was so glad he had taken her to gun ranges.

It would take time for Ramírez to jack up the camper, especially with it leaning. He would have to give the mechanical issue total attention.

Looking around, he saw the remnants of a house that had been vacated long ago. Indians who follow traditional native religions believe that when a person dies in a house, the witch doctor must come and cast out evil spirits.

They willingly pay whatever fee the witch doctor decides, which can be thousands of dollars. Without the fee, the witch doctor curses the house. The house is considered to have a death spirit and must be vacated and abandoned Those who believe the witch doctor fear tragedy if they even enter the abandoned building.

Ramírez hastened inside the ruins to make sure there were no wild animals, snakes, or spiders. His wife did not like spiders. They found a place where she could sit, prop the rifle and not be seen from the road.

He went to work on the camper. He was tightening the last bolt on the spare tire when they heard the whine of an engine being driven at high speed. A car burst into view and stopped abruptly about 50 yards from the camper.

Two men jumped out of the car with guns drawn and yelled for Ramírez to get on the ground. The tone of their voices was not friendly. They meant harm.

As he was getting to the ground, he yelled loudly: "You might want to reconsider; you are being watched."

These words were a signal to his wife. She blasted two shots and two tires of the car behind the gunmen exploded, dropping the rims to the asphalt.

They hesitated, surprised. This had not been part of the plan. They had known Ramírez was traveling with his wife, but they did not know she was a dead shot with a rifle. They also did not know from which direction the shots came.

There was the sound of another car coming. It stopped behind the men holding guns aimed at Ramírez. Four Navajos seemed to catapult from the second car. They disappeared in separate directions.

What Ramírez had not known was that the Navajo at the campsite had put a tracking device on his vehicle. They were never far away from Ramírez and his wife.

It was a stalemate. Ramírez with hands in the air. Two men with guns drawn on Ramírez and the driver in the car. Four Navajos somewhere. And a woman with a rifle and a keen hand on the trigger.

With a command for the two gunmen in the road to drop their weapons all four Navajos fired warning shots. The two gunmen and the driver of the car realized they were surrounded.

Guns were dropped. A Navajo stepped into the open and cautiously approached to collect the weapons. With a deft motion of hand, one by one, he left three men unconscious.

With three Navajos still hidden, the fourth Navajo walked up to Ramírez and said: "Get squaw and leave!"

Ramírez called to his wife. While his wife was running toward the camper, Ramírez was carefully backing the camper onto the roadway. With his wife inside, he pushed the RPMs. They lurched forward, leaving behind three men who would wish they had never seen a Navajo.

Ramírez did not look back. He did reflect on a story of what had happened to a white man who had gone uninvited to a squaw dance. One could not help but have a twinge of pity even for evil persons falling into the hands of offended native Indians. Death could be wished for long before it became a reality.

THIRTY-SIX

Trouble awakened to the smell of freshly cooked food. Deer, duck, and rabbit had been slowly turned on spits over fires burning dry hickory wood. Goat's milk, cheese, and bread were sitting on a rock ledge.

A group of Navajo warriors sat with their legs crossed facing a man whose hair had long ago turned from grey to white. Trouble was arrested by the scene. The silence was not forced, yet it was binding, a voluntary silence, not of worship but awe.

Trouble came to know the man sitting cross-legged as the Ancient One. There was no other name for him. The last generation had called him the Ancient One. The generation before that had called him the Ancient One.

No one knew how old he was. No one asked. If they had asked, no one would have known. He had outlived anyone who lived when he was born.

If the Ancient One had been asked his age, he could not have told. There were no records of when he was born. Birth was a part of nature. Birthdays were not celebrated. Perhaps it was winter, or summer . . . maybe in time of snow or rain.

Why keep time? Life was one with nature. To be was the essence of life. Life is a gift from the Great Spirit. Man knows not the time when he shall return to the Creator.

To survive is the burden of a people. Individualism is submissive to the welfare of the community. To die is natural, not a thing of grief, but an act designed by the Great Spirit.

Only a few warriors knew that the Ancient One still lived. He was guarded night and day. Transport to different safe places was done by methods that would have baffled military experts. He had never spent a night under the roof of a man-made home. Caves or dugouts in sides of mountains were his native home. He spoke of teepees as places of community, not dwelling.

He told stories of things past lost in a timeless warp not binding listeners to clocks and calendars.

His words did not form sentences. A phrase might refer to an event, a hundred years, or a millennium. A word might be spoken and minutes pass. Every expression fell upon the ears of those present as more precious than life itself. Adverbs, adjectives, and verbs were few. He wore a breechcloth. His skin was like leather, yet with few wrinkles.

White hair flowed to his shoulders, outlining an angular face. His hands were folded on his lap.

His eyes like magnets drew others to him. Looking into them was to look into times and places that no longer existed—pools of water, deep blue, and unfathomable in depth. To the warriors, it seemed that the wisdom of those eyes could see into their very souls.

He had long ago understood that the Great Spirit had left him on earth to imbue to true warriors their mission. His life was fragile, but his mission compelled him.

Folks who had taken on white man's ways did not know of his existence. There were no pictures of him at Earl's and no need to ask for one. There were no pictures of him anywhere.

Trouble was called back to the need for food by his stomach growling. He ate heartily, while thinking city food never tasted so good.

He took his place beside the other warriors, sitting crosslegged as warriors do.

They sat in silence until the fires burned low. The only light was from a burning torch stuck in the wall of rock.

In the silence, the scratching of a mouse's feet could be heard. There was the faint tick-tick of a cricket as it hopped across the sandstone surface. There was a flickering sound of flames from the torch light. Then the whispering voice of the Ancient One.

He spoke of the Long Walk as if it were yesterday, and he was there. He spoke of times and spirits when there were no man-made machines. Wisdom was in his voice as he shared about the Great Spirit creating all things. He whispered of things not written, and things not in books, and things not heard in classrooms.

Warriors sat immobile. They were not hypnotized. They were not under the influence of peyote. They were fully conscious. They breathed deeply and softly to not disturb or lose a single word.

The Ancient One spoke of the Creator planning for a native people, noble of spirit, who would live by and of the earth. He spoke of things present and to come.

There were times that Trouble wondered whether the Ancient One's lips were moving. Did the sounds come from him like a ventriloquist? Or did the presence of the Ancient One communicate messages that seemed to be spoken?

Charismatic would not have been appropriate to describe the Ancient One. This was not just charisma of a personality, but the essence of a soul.

The torch on the wall burned low and died. Warriors did not move. It seemed an infinity passed. Another fire was lighted. The Ancient One was gone.

It seemed surreal. Trouble wondered if it had been a dream. Could a man live so long? Hunger pains made clear he was awake, and he was in a cave with warriors whose names he knew.

Warriors disappeared so subtly that Trouble was surprised to realize only those who had traveled with him were still present.

Two more days were spent resting and waiting for further instructions. Never a word was spoken by any warrior about the Ancient One. Yet time in the presence of the Ancient One had profoundly charged the atmosphere.

No one ventured to the area where the Ancient One had sat. He was not an idol, a god, or even considered a spirit. He did represent the spirit of who they were and would be as a native people.

THIRTY-SEVEN

They were deep in a forest. Two men and $6 million, but not too deep for others to know where they were. Others who were friendly.

There was the sound of a small engine. A gyrocopter whizzed by just over the treetops. A package was dropped with perfect timing into a small opening in the forest.

A change of clothes, map, two Browning 1911 pistols with a generous amount of bullets, and new Ohio driver's licenses—one for each of them—were in the bag. A GPS was preset for a time and meeting place.

It would take two days traveling through the forest to arrive on a flat-topped rocky knoll on the edge of the wilderness. A photo had been included of the meeting place.

They arrived an hour early and found a hiding place in the event of unfriendly visitors.

With perfect timing, a Sikorsky S-76C helicopter landed. A secret signal indicating all was clear came from the copter. The two Navajos were swiftly aboard with the $6 million. Landing and liftoff were incredibly quick.

Their destination was a remote rural area in southern Ohio, leaving enough fuel for the Sikorsky to fly 50 miles. They bathed and changed clothes on the helicopter. Dressed in executive suits, they left the money on the chopper.

Their duty was done. A car was waiting. They headed west.

The Navajos on the chopper were responsible to transport the money to where it would be transferred to an international account. The helicopter had been rented through a shell company with false passports. It would be returned wiped down. No trace would be left pointing to Navajos.

The last of the stones were sold, and all the money was safe. The plan could move to the next stage.

THIRTY-EIGHT

Syed had every intention of heading to Sydney. He did not know that he was being hunted.

The ship that had slipped out of dock in Burma had joined with another ship and had been tracking Syed. The night that Syed's ship had turned flood lights on clandestine behaviors had not been forgiven. There was concern Syed's ship may have taken pictures or gained knowledge of the contraband being illegally shipped.

Pirates had sunk their partner's ship that was searching for Syed. The ship that had slipped out of the harbor in Burma witnessed the sinking, knowing that valuable documents were at risk. Via drone they had been able to observe cargo and items being salvaged by the pirates. There was contraband hidden in the cargo.

Syed's ship had encountered the pirates in a fatal battle and recovered cargo and weapons from the pirate boat.

The cartel ship was following Syed in hopes of recovering what had been taken from the pirate ship and then sinking Syed's ship. There was no knowledge of Syed's ship having been retrofitted. It just looked like a fancy cargo vessel.

Two days out of East Timor, Syed was awakened with a call from the quartermaster. A ship without a flag was on the horizon and coming directly toward them at full speed.

Syed hastened to the command center, still in slippers and robe. The first mate knew what to do to prepare crew and deck.

Syed went into battle plan. He had a feeling that this was the ghost ship of their visit to Burma. No chances would be taken.

He pressed a button and walls of bulletproof steel rose up to surround the command center. A periscope provided visibility. Shafts of bullet-resistant steel slid up along the deck to protect vital items and sensitive materials.

Syed made a tactical decision. He asked the engine room for three-quarter speed and headed directly toward the oncoming ship. That would surprise the other captain who probably assumed Syed's ship was nothing more than an unarmed merchant ship.

When clearly in sight of the other ship, but a safe distance away, Syed reduced speed, filled a ballast to 20 percent of capacity, and made a hard turn starboard. In a series of maneuvers that had been carefully tested in trial runs, Syed tacked the ship and then reversed the procedure to port. He was coming directly toward the side of the other ship.

Syed pressed another button and a bonus from Israeli friends rose up from its hiding place. It was an electromagnetic railgun with laser locked into place. The U.S. military was still testing the weapon. Israel wanted to know if the technology worked in real battle. They had agreed to set up the gun on Syed's ship if they could install remote cameras to observe via satellite. Israeli experts would be watching.

The other ship was caught totally by surprise. How could a ship loaded with cargo do starboard and port with such speed? To keep Syed's ship from passing behind, they cut their speed. It was a fatal mistake.

Syed slowed speed, but kept engines humming in the event there should be a surprise. He did not know what weapons the other ship might have, and he did not intend to wait to find out.

He pressed a button. The railgun moved slightly to the right. Seconds later with target located, the gun was fired.

It does not take long for a 23-pound projectile to travel 4,000 feet at 5,000 mph. The hit was direct mid-ship just above the water line, apparently severing a fuel line. The explosion was instantaneous and disastrous.

There would be no need to worry about further battle. The ship would sink. Every man alive would be jumping into a life raft. Flames had risen quickly to engulf the command center and the communications center. No distress signal would be sent.

Only two of Syed's men were above deck. He retracted the railgun. Better to keep some things quiet.

Now the wait. He would not leave men to drown, no matter how evil they were. But he would not risk his ship and men.

In a moment of reflection, he thought about the Israelis who would have observed via satellite the railgun focus and fire. One bullet essentially destroyed a ship, wreaking havoc and ending a battle. They would be pleased. They would also be impressed by the performance of his ship to position for battle. He was glad for friends.

Mid-morning the ship sank into the waters. Two lifeboats were slowly making their way toward Syed's ship.

He decided that it would be a good idea to equip a few of his men with the AK-47s captured from the pirates. Still he was not in a hurry. Patience on the high seas is directly related to survival.

It was late morning when the lifeboats came near enough for communication. Syed's quartermaster lined eight of his men up along the deck, each armed with an AK-47. They looked fierce, though half of the guns were not loaded. It is not a good idea to give a man a loaded gun when he has never held one in his hands.

A man from the lifeboats called out. Only one of Syed's crew had a basic understanding of the language. The order was given for the men in the lifeboats to strip of all clothing. They would have no item with them when lifted one by one into a net to the deck of the ship. No ladder would be extended.

No chances were to be taken. They would come aboard five minutes between each rescue.

If any man being brought aboard attempted violence, he was to be thrown overboard near the life rafts. If they resisted, they would not be killed, but they would be left to the vicissitudes of a life raft, winds, and waves.

As each man came aboard, he was given a blanket. Syed had no intention of cruelty. The plan was to protect his men and ship.

One of the nine men rescued seemed to be the leader, though it was not apparent if his authority was formal or a group acceptance. They appeared to be of the same ethnicity.

Syed was a leader of men. He wanted information, but there would be time. The men were to shower and be given clothes. It was more than their body odor. What they could have in their hair or on their bodies was too great of a risk to the crew. Sanitation on Syed's ship was held to high standards.

When the men were brought back to the main deck in clean clothes, they were stunned to see a table with ten chairs, linen cloth, and silverware. They were directed to sit, leaving an empty chair at the head of the table. Food served was generous and chef quality.

Oddly, every man dropped his head. There was a quiet mumbling by one of the nine. Until he stopped speaking, no one looked up.

Captain Syed was observing. He had never seen such behavior. Men were hungry. Why did they wait? What was being said by the person mumbling?

He determined to know more.

Captain Syed's men stood in discreet places, alert, with guns, yet not threatening. The AK-47s they carried were sufficient intimidation.

Meal finished, the nine men were led to a cabin large enough for them and with its own restroom. The door was secured from the outside.

For three days, twice each day, the men were allowed to come to the table and enjoy a full meal. Not a word was spoken to them. However, Syed took note that each time they came to the table, they bowed their heads and one of them mumbled.

On the fourth day as the men came to the main deck to eat, Captain Syed was standing at the tenth chair in his full-dress uniform. Syed's crewman who knew a little of the language would try to translate.

The men were seated and instructed to eat. After the time of bowed heads, Syed began with questions which he directed to individuals. He would know if they were being consistent.

Their story unfolded with candidness, humility, and consistency. They were Kachin tribe from Myanmar. The Buddhist government violently persecuted their people because they were Christians—a product of a Baptist missionary in the 1850s. Second, the ancestral land of the Kachin tribe is rich with jade, precious jewels, and oil.

About 50 Kachin men had been kidnapped and sold into slavery. After two years of brutal training only a small number were alive. Thirteen of them had been on the ship that sank. The nine at the table were the only survivors. The ship they had been on had been intended to be their home until their death, whether killed by their captors, dying naturally, by accident, or in battle. They would never have been on land again had Syed not rescued them.

Again, and again, the men thanked Captain Syed for saving their lives. Their candor and sincerity were moving and convincing.

Syed decided to keep the men quarantined. His men would be tense if men rescued from a sinking pirate ship were allowed freedom of deck. He would decide what to do with them upon arrival in Sydney.

Their food would be the same as the crew for the rest of the trip, but served to their quarters. Two at a time, they would be allowed daily exercise on deck.

Syed was a wise captain. He knew men. He knew that character cannot be hidden. What a man is he will do.

THIRTY-NINE

The old bomb of a truck's engine was humming sweetly when by moonlight Trouble and the warriors with him ran several hundred yards and jumped in. They would be passing through Gallup as folks were coming to the streets early morning. The timing was intentional.

Three miles from Gallup the driver pressed a button. The engine went into a limp mode, like a spark plug was misfiring. A special module kicked in creating an ugly stream of white smoke. Mechanics would shake their heads and say "blown head gasket." Other folks would look without envy at the old truck as a relic soon destined for a scrap heap or junkyard.

No one would suspect that a young Asian boy looking like a Navajo and speaking their language would be inside the vehicle. Those who had been part of the mission had shared no secrets. If the old truck had been previously seen it had offered no clue to Preacherman and Trouble's presence on the reservation.

Five miles out of Gallup, the driver released buttons. The throbbing of the engine thrust it forward to lead traffic. Albuquerque was soon behind them as they headed east, too fast to count the windmills on the distant ridges.

Inside the old bomb of a truck the dashboard looked a lot like an airplane engine cockpit. There were radars for weather, for traffic, and for police cars. Buttons pressed changed stop lights, allowing the truck to keep rolling.

Satellite helped them to know where trains and airplanes were. The FBI, perturbed by the disastrous failed raid on the reservation, was spreading a wide net of surveillance.

When the old truck passed other vehicles, many drivers shook their head as if they expected the bucket-of-bolts to fall apart in the middle of the road. What they saw on the outside was in strong contrast to what was on the inside.

It was not long after lunchtime when they rolled into Little Rock, Arkansas.

The destination was an outlying farm. They drove the truck into a barn. Doors closed behind them.

A pit crew that would have been envied by Nascar was waiting. New body parts with bullet-resistant metal began to form a modified vehicle with classic, yet unique features. The high gloss black color was so deep it looked like a mirror. New tires were resistant to puncture, designed for 25 miles after being pierced.

Another crew welded a box on the back that blended in so smoothly it appeared to be part of the body. There was mystery inside the box.

Meanwhile, Trouble's hair was cut, and he was dressed in the tailored clothes that had been prepared for him. He rode into the barn looking like a warrior. He would ride out looking like a very rich teenager.

Work done, they ate and rested. Plans were discussed. From this point on, Trouble would participate in all decisions.

It was after midnight when the barn doors opened and the truck drove into the night. A Navajo was at the wheel. They would be arriving at the new home on Long Island in time for dinner.

The rest of the trip all speed limits would be obeyed. No chances would be taken.

If the Feds were looking for an old truck, it would not be found.

FORTY

Ramírez was first to rise and went as usual to make coffee. A piece of paper had been slipped through the window behind the coffee maker.

He unfolded the paper and read it before waking his wife. The code given to them at the campground included further instructions. They were about 200 miles from Long Island.

They were to drive to a scenic lookout and park the camper. After being parked for a few minutes, they were to leave the camper, take a walk, and return to the parking lot arriving at the opposite end. A green Lexus would be parked in the first parking space.

Ramírez and his wife were to casually get into the Lexus and drive away without looking back. Cash would be under the seat for any needs they might have. Any personal items in the camper would be delivered to them. The camper would be returned to its owner with a generous gift.

The GPS in the Lexus was preset for their destination. When they arrived at the gated community, the remote control opened the VIP gate. They did not stop.

Arrival at the destination revealed a grand mansion backed up to water and surrounded by rock walls of exquisite design. A Navajo butler waited to usher them to their quarters, and a Navajo valet parked the car.

Ramírez and his wife had been advised that Trouble was to arrive in time for dinner. Mrs. Ramírez headed for the kitchen which was a woman's dream. The cupboards were full. Soon the savory aroma of food seeped out of the kitchen to other areas of the house.

A decision had been made to allow no outside help. Ramírez's wife would provide meals. Navajos would help with serving and housekeeping. There would be guards 24/7.

The mission was clear. FBI and bad people were looking for Preacherman and Trouble. Trouble and Preacherman were looking for bad people. They hoped to be under the radar with the FBI until their mission was accomplished.

Mrs. Ramírez remembered the time Preacherman and Trouble had come to their home. Thinking of foods men would like who had not eaten homestyle in a long time, she was busy, humming to herself. While preparing the main meal, she began a variety of delicacies. The oven was busy.

FORTY-ONE

Preacherman had been in New York City for several days to ensure that plans were orderly and secure. At the time Ramírez and his wife arrived, he was opening a bank account and depositing a Swiss check for $7million. There would be deposits in other banks with funds being directed through the mining company in Australia.

In a few days, he would be traveling to the Navajo Reservation for a meeting with Indian Bureau officials, the president, vice president, and other officials. Either they would cooperate, or he would direct reservation funds to Sioux, Blackfoot, Hopi, or other tribes.

Navajos were not the only tribe that had needs. Alcoholism, teenage pregnancy, and unemployment were blights to most of the reservations. He would refuse to be bribed or manipulated. He and Trouble had made a promise to the Navajo warriors. They would keep their promise.

The funds would not be deposited to the Bureau of Indians for distribution. Men and women Preacherman had chosen would manage the funds and direct the projects, providing water and other amenities to reservation families.

Too many native Indians still lived without water and electricity.

FORTY-TWO

The chauffeur for Trouble had been a career military driver for colonels. He had insisted on assignment to battle zones. Generals wanted him as their driver, but he threatened leaving the military if transferred. Generals were too far back in the safe zone. He loved risk.

More than a few times, his driving abilities had saved the lives of every person in a military vehicle. His job now was to drive the truck and do whatever was needed to protect Preacherman and Trouble. He knew every inch of the truck, its power, breaking ability, and the maximum tilt on two wheels.

He also knew every secret of the truck's resources that could be useful in a crisis. Certain weapons were programmed to voice command. No need to press buttons. Navajo code words could bring about remarkable action instantly.

On the civil side, it was a fancy vehicle deserving to transport high society folks. In line with Rolls-Royces, Lamborghinis, and other luxury vehicles at a Five-Star event, it would be the truck that would be envied.

On the not-so-civil side, unfriendly folks would discover the truck to be a formidable foe.

FORTY-THREE

Kahlil was finding himself increasingly living a lonely life in his home. Courtesy was extended to him. Family was civil. Dinners were an exercise in politeness and small talk, ignoring the giant elephant in the room.

He sensed that news of events related to Rahel was being shared commonly in his house. Try as he might, he could not get even a whisper of why there seemed to be a growing atmosphere of hope.

Azian's business ventures were becoming increasingly profitable, which decreased Azian's available time to assist Kahlil. Khalil found his workload heavy, travel less frequent, and hiring reliable assistants difficult.

Life had become a dreadful routine. Money and power had lost their fascination. When those closest to you no longer desire to be around, even a kingdom becomes a prison. Luxury does not replace friendship and love. Power does not buy love.

Kahlil was a lonely man. Loneliness had driven him to desperation. His scouts had been able to trace some of the trips of Azian. He had learned of Azian's meeting with Rahel's in-laws.

The night was long and with little sleep. He made a decision, but decided he would not tell his wife or anyone. Early in the morning the family chauffeur drove him to the city. He sent the chauffeur on an errand to dismiss him and drove to the airport. He bought a first-class ticket to England's Heathrow Airport in London.

He was going to visit Stewart's parents.

FORTY-FOUR

The truck rumbled through the gates and up to the mansion, not slowing down until it was in an underground concrete garage. Trouble and a Navajo stepped into an elevator for the ride up to the main floor.

When the elevator door opened, the aroma of freshly cooked food gnawed at their stomachs. Food was prepared and ready to be served. The butler directed them to the restrooms to freshen up.

The elevator door opened again, and Preacherman stepped out.

Ramírez was helping his wife. The two of them seemed to be in the seventh heaven of happiness.

When Trouble entered the dining room, Ramírez's wife almost dropped hot rolls at the sight of him. The night he and Preacherman had left their home, he was a stripling of a boy. How could he have changed so much in such a short time? He had become a young man, pounds heavier, deeper skin tone, dressed immaculately, handsome, keen-eyed, and charming.

She recovered her composure.

Dinner was served.

Ramírez took note she tended to stay near Trouble. He knew her heart. She would die for the boy. Trouble had become her reason for living. Her dreams of a son rested in Trouble.

FORTY-FIVE

The next few days were quiet and peaceful with the exception of daily meetings between Trouble and Preacherman. There were scheduled meetings with the warriors to evaluate security.

Thus far, there had not been a ripple of rumor picked up on the streets to suggest even association between the rich folks from Australia and Preacherman and Trouble. But there was a buzz about the secrecy of the mansion.

Work on an underground tunnel from the basement garage to the waterway was being completed. The opening of the tunnel would be under a pier. A yacht attached to the pier was kept ready. A guard was always on duty in a tower to protect the yacht and rear of the mansion.

A battle plan was being devised. It was time to take the battle to the bad guys.

FORTY-SIX

Captain Syed had hoped to see Stewart while in Australia, but Stewart was in New York City. When Syed arrived at Stewart's Australian corporate offices, there was a message for him to use Stewart's secure line for a conference call with Stewart and Alaina.

Syed was directed to a guest suite for executives in the corporate office. The video conference was in progress, and Stewart was on the screen.

Syed's first question was to ask about Rahel's son. Answering him, Stewart confirmed that a DNA test had verified the exhumed body was that of his wife, Rahel.

However, there were no public records of the boy. If he were alive, there was no knowledge of his location. None of their sources had been able to offer any information that would be helpful to find the boy.

Syed shared with Stewart about sinking the pirate boat and the ship. He told about taking nine prisoners. He held into the camera one of the papers from the satchel taken from the pirates.

There was a gasp as Alaina exclaimed:

"Captain, hold that steady. I know that language. It was spoken by my grandmother. My grandfather was military, and they lived five years among the people who speak that language. My grandfather led 300 Kachin warriors in battle against 10,000 Japanese in World War II. Grandmother diligently taught me the language, pretending it was a game. I am a little rusty, but I can try to translate."

Page by page, Syed held the notes before the camera for Alaina to take photos. She promised to immediately begin translation.

Stewart and Syed discussed the cargo that had been taken from the pirate ship and decided to store it in one of the corporate warehouses. Stewart explained that a new customer who owned a gold mine in Australia wanted a special shipment made to New York City. Stewart wanted the shipment to be excellently done to secure the business relationship.

They discussed the nine prisoners. Captain Syed shared that some of them had been trained with weapons. He was of the opinion they had told the truth about being kidnapped and forced to serve on a pirate ship.

He told Stewart about the fear the Kachins had of being sent back to their own country.

Stewart suggested that five of them be housed in a secure area. They could be employed while processing documentation. It would be a test. If they were honest they would be afraid to leave. The four who were best with weapons could remain with Syed on the ship.

They agreed to talk after Alaina had translated some of the papers. Meanwhile, Syed would have transferred the cargo and prepared to sail the ship.

Syed returned to the ship to meet with the Kachins. When he shared with them Stewart's suggestion, they readily accepted. Their expressions of gratitude were heartwarming.

Paperwork and meetings with port authorities consumed the next few hours. It was difficult for Syed to concentrate on immediate duties. Always there was the subconscious hope for the boy. What would Alaina discover in the documents recovered from the pirate ship?

Whatever he may have imagined, the truth was more shocking.

The documents were instructions from a cartel for the boy in the airport video to be found and eliminated. There was a reference to a Navajo Indian who had been associated with the boy and seen in the same area where members of the cartel had been killed. Evidence suggested the Navajo man and the boy might be aware of cartel plans or even have information of cartel operations, including names to the highest level.

The boy had seen computers with sensitive information and been present in numerous areas of cartel action. In a particular confrontation with the Navajo and the boy, a large box of uncut precious stones had disappeared.

Further instructions revealed that a certain captain and his ship might be privy or even be in possession of papers about international cartel operations. The captain and his ship were to be destroyed. The ship was en route to New York City. Instructions were given to bomb and sink the ship in the harbor. The captain was to be kidnapped or killed.

Stewart, Alaina, and Captain Syed talked long. They decided it would be wise to share all they knew with Jeb and seek his counsel.

FORTY-SEVEN

The tunnel had been completed. The night before, Preacherman and one of the guards had exited through the tunnel to the shore, slipped into the boat, and took it for a trial run on the East River.

The objective was to test time to exit the tunnel, get into the boat, leave the dock house, and get a half mile into the river. Total time was 4 minutes and 23 seconds. They were pleased.

FORTY-EIGHT

Alaina had suggested to Jeb that he and Azian should meet casually. Jeb's home would be a great place. The intent was to give the appearance of a social visit.

Jeb's children were outside playing in the yard when Azian arrived by taxi. He had dressed casually. As he stepped into the yard, a soccer ball came flying in his direction. He deftly kicked it back to the oldest boy. The children insisted he play with them.

Azian was still in the yard kicking a soccer ball when Jeb got off the city transit bus. They entered the house with the children surrounding Azian like a favorite uncle who had come to visit.

The grill was in the backyard in view of neighbors. From time to time, one of the children would throw a frisbee or softball at Azian. The evening was casual with lots of laughter.

Jeb's sister-in-law, Ari, a senior at the University of Virginia law school was home for spring break. Azian took note that she did not have a wedding band, but she did have personality, intelligence, and was gorgeous. For the first time, his eyes and heart were captured.

As had been planned, Azian shared what he knew about Rahel and her son in the mix of the conversation and dinner. Azian took note that Ari stayed near enough to hear. He wanted to believe that she was curious about him. Jeb shared nothing; he just listened.

Before sunset, they all walked with Azian down the sidewalk to catch a taxi. It was like a family "goodbye."

Azian was not sure what had been accomplished in the search for his nephew, but he would be in touch with Jeb and ask for Ari's phone number.

What Azian did not know was that Ari was specializing in studies of investigative law. She would be having a long discussion with Jeb, offering possibilities of how to find the boy.

FORTY-NINE

The ship was loaded. Captain Syed had one more meeting—the sheik whose daughter had been rescued from the pirates had arrived.

They had decided to rent a suite in a five-star hotel. The hotel would provide security. Each of them would bring two or three men with sharp eyes and tactical skills as security guards.

The suite had a large meeting room and numerous bedrooms. They would spend the night with food catered to them and have plenty of time to talk.

Each had tried to learn as much as possible about the other before meeting. Both were satisfied that character was impeccable and trustworthy.

As the evening progressed, they became more casual in conversation sharing personal sides of their lives, their loves, and their fortunes—-no talk about money, but lots of talk about adventures.

Syed alluded to the story of the Arab girl who had fled her country because of being pregnant. He talked as if it were a story he had heard. What he said was vague, yet the sheik took note and pressed for details.

Syed shared that he believed the woman had a child who was still alive. He held in reserve vital pieces of information about his personal part in the story of Rahel. He was inclined to trust the sheik, but caution is the character of a sea captain. Tides can wash up on shore secrets long thought lost or forgotten.

The sheik rose and walked to a window looking out over the bay. He stood silent for some time. Syed thought he was just enjoying the scenery. It was a respectful silence.

The sheik turned and said: "I may know of this situation involving the young woman. If she is who I think she is, my company has done business with her father. He is noted for his arrogance and sometimes ruthless power."

There was further silence. The sheik continued: "I owe you a great debt, greater than I can ever repay. You saved my yacht, but the yacht is only a boat. What is more important, you saved my daughter's life and the lives of my crew. I will do what I can to help you."

It was after 2 a.m. when they finally retired. Still Syed did not tell about Stewart, his taking Rahel to the United States, or the hotel owner who had first kept Rahel and her son.

The following morning they established a method of communication before going their separate ways. Syed's ship left for New York City with cargo from an Australian gold and mineral miner.

Though Syed did not know that the cartel was tracking him with negative plans for his future, he was thankful that he had brought the four Kachin men rescued from the pirate boat. Their training had been excellent. They were first-class sailors and seemed to have an eye for anything that needed attention. One of them was an exceptional mechanic. One had an eye to the deck, making sure everything was in its proper place, clean, and in working order.

He had a feeling the Kachins would come in mighty handy before the journey was finished.

FIFTY

Breakfast over, Mrs. Ramírez explained that sandwiches would be available in the parlor for lunch. The kitchen and dining room were off limits until 5 p.m., at which time, everyone was to meet in the parlor prepared to enter.

She dismissed them as if they were a bunch of schoolboys and headed for the kitchen.

As promised, there were sandwiches for lunch, but it was difficult to enjoy a sandwich with the savory aromas drifting from the kitchen. There were whispers as to the mystery. Only Preacherman and the Ramírez couple knew.

It was a long afternoon. At the appointed time, everyone gathered in the parlor. Preacherman was with them. Officer Ramírez shared that they were to enter with Preacherman being first and Trouble being last.

When Trouble came through the door, they began to sing "Happy Birthday!" The room was decorated with a mix of Navajo and Asian party favors.

Preacherman explained that Trouble's adoption papers had been finalized. A date of birth had been necessary for adoption papers and, since no date of birth was known, today had been declared as his fourteenth birthday.

Trouble sat at one end of the table, and Preacherman at the other. For a little while, the room was silent as they enjoyed the food and delicacies.

While Trouble looked impassive, inside there was a churning of emotions. It seemed like a dam had broken and waters were flooding. There were no tears, but his heart was constricted and his pulse was pounding.

He finally spoke: "I do not know how to tell you your place in my life. Each of you has become the only family I have ever known, except my mother. I am grateful!"

What followed were nervous shuffling, strange coughing, and more than a few eyes moist with tears. Mrs. Ramírez hastened toward the kitchen, not for the sake of food, but privacy.

FIFTY-ONE

Kahlil was received graciously by Stewart's parents. However, it was unnerving for Kahlil to be in a secondary posture. The humbling was not a result of the way he was received or treated.

Kahlil knew wealth and power. What he did not know was the character that comes with a family whose roots are hundreds of years deep. Portraits of sea captains, lords, barons, princesses, and famous historical persons hung on walls. He had read about many of them.

The home was distinguished, not dated, yet not modern. It tastefully spoke of having served generations of the same family; it displayed great wealth, without being ostentatious—a feeling that character was more important than possessions.

It was Kahlil's first time to be in a Christian home. He noticed portraits that had biblical names—some names were familiar from his religion. He passed a small chapel with a Bible open on a podium. He knew that it was a Bible, though he did not know what was in the book.

The manner of his hosts was without pretense; it was presumed wealth and power. The statement was in the presence.

Graciousness extended courtesy. Servants were relaxed, yet attentive. It occurred to Kahlil that those who were serving had no fear and enjoyed their work.

What most surprised Kahlil was the personal reception. They knew he was Rahel's father and knew some of the story. Yet there was a kindness about them that baffled Kahlil. He assumed they did not know of his anger against Rahel.

A wedding portrait of Stewart and Rahel was among family portraits displayed. Kahlil gasped at the beauty of Rahel and the happiness that was written in her eyes.

The portrait had been commissioned by Stewart's parents when he had shared with them about marriage to Rahel. The artist had worked from a photo.

Kahlil was thinking. Stewart had married without his parents' presence. He had married an Asian woman. Stewart's parents had accepted the marriage as Stewart's decision. This was culture that Kahlil had not experienced.

Stewart's parents shared with Kahlil that they understood why the wedding was quiet and private. They would have liked to have been in attendance, but Stewart had explained to them that privacy was necessary and preferred by his bride.

"Anyway," Stewart's mom said, "He would never have been happy with a pomp-and-splendor wedding."

With candor, they shared what they knew with Kahlil. Rahel had died in the United States. She had a son that may still be alive. Efforts were being made to find the boy as soon as possible, because it was believed the boy's life could be in danger.

They explained that Stewart was making an aggressive effort to find his son.

"As grandparents, we have assured Stewart that no resources will be spared until our grandson is found," Stewart's father said.

They did not share details about Azian's part in the search, though Kahlil was beginning to understand some of the strange happenings of the past.

He left Stewart's parents' home stunned by the differences between his culture and their culture. He had run his family like a business.

His religion had been forced upon everyone in the household. What folks believed in their hearts was irrelevant to him so long as they kept the religious customs and did not violate his home with any other religion.

He thoughtfully mused that his religion was more about culture, while Stewart's family religion was more about heart and attitude. His religion stacked people up in terms of power and prestige. This new religion valued people as equals.

His perception had been that people are weak. They need authority. He had been the authority. The idea of individual human dignity had never occurred to him before this visit.

His mind was in shock. Rahel was dead. He had a grandson who might be alive and in danger. Stewart's parents had graciously received him without malice or ill will. He had never before experienced wealthy and powerful people treating servants as equals.

A revolution was taking place in his heart.

FIFTY-TWO

With Azian gone and the family retired for the evening, Ari made Jeb feel like he was in a courtroom on a witness stand. She fired question after question, asking for nothing that would violate his professional duties. She doggedly pressed him for analysis. Many questions needed only a "Yes," "No," or one-word answer. She was skillfully weaving sentences together for her argument with the jury.

The clock ticked until after midnight when Jeb practically jumped out of his chair. "The warehouse," he exclaimed. "The warehouse! It must be primary in what is happening in the United States."

Ari just smiled. The jury was in. The verdict was rendered. She had won her case.

The warehouse was pivotal.

Jeb would know what to do. He would need no instructions.

FIFTY-THREE

A decision was made for Officer Ramírez and his wife to visit the police headquarters. Inevitably, Officer Ramirez would be seen and recognized. Better that it appears that he and his wife had taken a soft retirement after their travels.

There would be no harm for others to think they were assisting a wealthy Australian and his son.

They rode the subway part of the way into the city, took a bus to within six blocks of the police department, and then motioned for a taxi. Timing was perfect. They had made an appointment to talk with the chief of police.

Ramírez was greatly surprised when doors opened that several high officials and more than a dozen ranking officers were present. His departure from the police department had been sudden, leaving no time for recognition of his distinguished service. A celebration of his retirement was in order.

There were comments by officials, commendations from the mayor for an impeccable record of performance, as well as plaques and awards. Cake was served.

When things quieted down, Ramírez's former captain asked if he would come by his office for a few minutes.

Ramírez did not know that the entire event had been staged to arrange for the captain to talk with him. High brass and the mayor do not show up for every retirement ceremony.

When the door closed behind Ramírez, the captain said: "Officer, I have always had great respect for you. You must know that I have evidence that you have been in contact with the boy in the airport video and the Navajo known in the streets as Preacherman."

The captain was hoping Ramírez would not ask questions. What he had was more hunches and theory than fact.

"Bluntly, let me share with you. We have not been able to find any evidence of the boy and the Navajo committing any crimes. At the present time, we have no idea whether they are dead or alive. We believe you know.

"This you must tell me. If they are alive, are they involved in any criminal activities? If you say 'No,' I will take your word for it. However, if we later find that they are guilty of collaborating with criminals, your years of good service will count for nothing. We will take you down with them. We will strip every honor you have ever received. If you live, you will be arrested and spend a long time in prison."

There was silence in the room. Ramírez tried to breathe deeply and slowly. He looked steadily at the captain and said:

"I will stake my life that the man and boy are innocent of crimes."

The captain took note that Ramírez's answer was given in a careful way. He had known Ramírez a long time. His reading of Ramírez's words, tone, and facial expression was that the officer knew a lot more than he was telling. Yet, the captain was satisfied that Ramírez did not believe the Navajo and boy were criminal.

FIFTY-FOUR

Tauranga was a day behind them. Captain Syed wanted to see New York City. The cargo was valuable, but light. The ship was not designed for cargo above the deck. Design was for small and valuable cargo to be delivered in less than normal time.

The powerful engines were pushing the ship at 26-28 knots. Syed reflected that his Israeli friends had done an incredible engineering job of retrofitting the ship. He loved his ship.

Dawn was slowly awakening. A mist hung over the ocean. All was well.

Captain Syed had just entered the command center when a distress signal was received. A ship's engines had failed. Satellite indicated Captain Syed's ship was by far the nearest to the distressed vessel.

No discussion was necessary. A change of course was set. It would take about 30 minutes to reach the vessel that had indicated engine failure.

The first mate gave instructions to the crew for all hands to be on deck. As a precaution, Syed instructed that several men were to be armed. A ship in distress cannot be ignored. However, the character of those on board a ship would have to be tested. It was better to be cautious.

When still far off, it became obvious that a man was standing on the deck of the distressed ship waving a flag.

At that moment, there was commotion on Syed's deck. One of the Kachin men was running toward the command center yelling at the top of his voice. Several of Syed's crew quickly restrained him. He made no resistance, but said in broken English: "Danger…speak …Captain…danger!" he frantically said over and over.

While he did not resist, there was fear in his eyes and he was shaking, sweating, and pointing to the ship with the distress flag being waved. He kept repeating,

"Danger! Danger!"

A translator shared the message with the first mate.

With firm hands locked on his arms he was taken directly to the command center. He spoke and a translator communicated his message: "Captain, it is a trick. I know that ship. They have guns and will attack when you approach. I have seen this done many times."

Captain Syed slowed his ship and moved starboard. Better to be safe than sorry. The other ship was not sinking. There would be no harm in delaying and investigating.

Taking binoculars, he carefully studied the other ship. He could easily see six areas that were suspect. He also thought it most peculiar that only a handful of men could be seen on deck. There was no evidence of fire, nor was there an obvious sign of the ship being in distress. Not a man was on deck attending issues that would have been normal for a distressed ship.

Slowly, he moved in a wide arc around the other vessel. He saw quick movement as a weapon was shifted behind a false front.

Convinced that the Kachin was telling the truth, Captain Syed gave instructions to release him. The look on his face and his hands raised in the air left Syed wondering who the Kachin was thanking.

Captain Syed had no heart to put another vessel on the ocean floor with perhaps innocent men aboard. He had not been able to forget that Kachin men who were innocent had gone down with the other ship. It was possible that Kachin men could be on this ship.

However, he could not leave them in a position to perhaps follow and do harm. He moved the ship a little more distant.

His decision was made. He pressed a button. A panel slid back. A gun with 3/4-mile range rose up and locked into position. A laser dot fixed on the aft part of the ship. The gun fired. The rudder of the enemy ship was disabled. It would take at least two days for repairs.

Captain Syed corrected course to New York City and decided to enjoy his ship. He gave a command for all men who wanted to stay above deck to take adequate precautions.

The ballasts filled, lifting the ship about two feet higher out of the water. The powerful engines for the next several hours thrilled sailors with an adventure they would tell their grandchildren. Several times they passed other ships with sailors rushing to the side rails astonished as if they were seeing a ghost ship.

If Captain Syed had a mistress, it was his ship.

FIFTY-FIVE

Stewart and Alaina walked casually down the streets of New York City. They were always mindful that others could be following. As they approached Times Square Church, they stepped out of the crowd and into the lobby. They had called ahead and made an appointment for a guided tour. Alaina was particularly interested in making a donation to the ministry working with homeless persons. It would also be a safe place to meet with Jeb and Azian.

She had seen the movie about the Rev. David Wilkerson winning gang member Nicki Cruz to Jesus. Later she had read about Reverend Wilkerson's intense work with homeless people. She knew that after the death of Reverend Wilkerson, the church had continued its mission to serve homeless and distressed people.

There was the assumption that a casual tour would make it very difficult for them to be followed. After the tour, they asked if they could sit in the balcony and wait for a Bible study to begin. People were filling up the lower floor.

Jeb eased in and took a seat, leaving two vacant spaces between him and Alaina. A few minutes later Azian sat down in the row in front of them.

Neither of them seemed to notice the other. Jeb held a Bible up in front of him as if he were reading and spoke softly.

"My sister-in-law, Ari, is an investigative lawyer. She has reviewed all evidence that we think could be associated with the boy and the Navajo. Ari is totally convinced that the warehouse where boxes fell on Stewart is central to operations in this city."

An usher passed by. Jeb asked if he could sit on the main floor near the front where the homeless people had reserved seats. Alaina had asked Jeb to observe the homeless and their response to the Bible study.

Jeb followed the usher without once glancing in the direction of Stewart, Alaina, or Azian. Azian drifted in another direction to exit the building. He would meet with Stewart and Alaina later and talk.

FIFTY-SIX

Captain Syed sent a coded message back to Stewart's corporate office in Sydney, sharing about the ship that had given a false distress signal. Considering the valuable cargo on his ship, he felt responsible to inform the company that had contracted him to deliver the cargo to New York City.

Corporate offices immediately forwarded the news from Captain Syed to Stewart.

Stewart put in a personal call to the gold miner who was his new Australian client, not realizing that the phone he was dialing was less than 20 miles away.

Preacherman answered his phone, and Stewart shared the news about the episode with what was apparently a pirate ship.

Preacherman asked many questions.

"Was anyone injured?"

"Is the cargo safe?"

"When will the ship arrive in the United States?"

"At which port will the ship dock?"

"What day is the projected arrival time?"

"Which warehouse will receive the goods?"

Preacherman asked if it would be possible for the ship to arrive at midnight on a certain day. He asked if he could meet the captain and pick up the two large suitcases that had been kept in the Captain's quarters. The rest of the cargo could be taken to the warehouse at 2 a.m.

The phone clicked and was silent.

Stewart thought it unusual for a wealthy person to take such an interest in particulars of shipping, but he reminded himself that the cargo had required a Lloyd's of London insurance policy of $25,000,000.

FIFTY-SEVEN

Jeb pondered the meeting with Azian, his wife, Stewart, and Alaina. He had not violated any law.

However, he was of the opinion that something big was coming down. If Ari was right about the warehouse, the FBI should be alerted. He could not as a Secret Service agent be involved without specific authorization.

Fortunately, he had a contact in the FBI. They had, in his younger days, worked together on a case involving the Mafia. While not friends, they did have mutual respect for each other.

Jeb called the FBI agent. He shared about his sister-in-law Ari helping to solve other crimes. Jeb shared Ari's firm belief that a certain warehouse could be pivotal to an international crime cartel.

The FBI contact did not make any commitments. However, as soon as he was off the phone, orders were given to secretly bug the warehouse and install a few strategically placed cameras that could be monitored remotely.

Agents were assigned the next day to secretly install listening devices and surveillance video in the warehouse.

FIFTY-EIGHT

Back at the mansion, a crew was intensely adding equipment to the truck and painting it satin black. Additional satellite equipment was added. All weapons were fully loaded and supplied with backup ammunition. Remote controls and firing mechanisms were double-checked to ensure they were operating flawlessly.

Trouble insisted that a few of his favorite Navajo weapons be added to the arsenal. He particularly wanted the non-returning boomerang and a bow and arrow that had been given to him on the day he became a brave. He would have a few darts which could come in handy in close quarters where silent offense was tactical.

He would also have a handcrafted, bone-handled, stainless steel knife. No warrior goes into battle without a knife.

Preacherman had saved his own life many times with a knife when in enemy territory during the war. He had taught Trouble every movement and trick of handling a knife to stay alive.

If the men were busy, the kitchen was busier. The Ramírez couple was having the time of their life cooking and keeping the house orderly.

Mrs. Ramírez insisted she take care of Trouble's room and clothes.

Trouble could only pull up vague memories of times with his mother. Mostly, he remembered her kindness, love, and things she had shared with him. While with his mother, they had lived minimally with survival being primary. Strangely, he did not think of the flat and time with his mother as lacking anything. There had been love.

The time between when he had left his mother to die in the flat and living in a mansion with wealth was surreal. His life was now surrounded with people. He was accepted as an equal.

He had sealed off part of his heart the day he said "goodbye" to his mother. He saw people as important and relationships as valuable. He knew there were good people and bad people. But he had not known intimacy and affection since his mother died.

While he knew that Preacherman would die for him, Preacherman had never hugged him or said any words of affection. The bond between them was inseparable and sensitive. But then Trouble had never had a father. He did not know what such a relationship should be.

He was bonded with the other Navajos. But the distance between his time with his mother and the present was an infinity. He had arrived on a distant shore. There was no emotional bridge to where he had sat on his mother's lap. She had run her fingers through his hair hugging him and saying words that warmed his heart and made him feel secure though they had lived in what others would call poverty.

His mother had cautioned him against becoming bitter, full of hatred, and selfish. Again and again, she had shared that regardless of how dark the day, he must believe that tomorrow the sun will shine.

"See the good," she would say, "and it will cover up all the bad. Focus on the good, and your heart will stay tender."

"You are a person. You are whole. You will live. You will grow up. You will one day find your dad. He was a man of faith who gently led me to see life with hope," she would say.

Preacherman had helped. When he could have been kidnapped or killed, Preacherman had rescued him. Now he was legally his father.

Preacherman did share with Trouble that he had arranged for the sale of half the precious stones to be invested in a business venture in Trouble's name. He did not share that Trouble would inherit the gold mine and his other assets. In addition, if he died before Trouble was of age, Trouble would receive military benefits through college—if he chose college.

But wealth to a boy who grew up in the streets is relative. He was prouder of his name, Sir Walter Scott, though it was a name he only carried in his heart. That which he held most dear was the medallion that would somehow lead him to his father.

Age 14, so the papers and birthday party said, he had become a young man. He thought about how it was to be living in a house with a woman always present. His clothes were kept impeccably clean, folded and ironed.

It was at nighttime when he found the covers of his bed always turned back that he had emotions he could not explain. How do you explain what you have not experienced or do not know?

While Trouble puzzled over Mrs. Ramírez's doting over him, no one else in the house seemed puzzled. It was more than a job. Her motherly instincts were at their best.

Officer Ramírez was a happy man. His wife was happy. With his happiness had come a new dimension to his life. At least once each week, he hung out with retired policemen who still had their fingers inside happenings of the police department.

He also had a couple of younger officers in uniform who kept their ears open.

Ramírez faithfully shared news he had gathered with Preacherman and Trouble, especially if there was a suggestion of cartel involvement. More and more fingers seemed to point to the warehouse.

FIFTY-NINE

Up in the penthouse, the huddle was intense with sweating and voices loud and angry. They were carefully tracking the ship from Australia. It was to arrive at midnight in the New York harbor.

The top level of the warehouse had been carefully designed to create an illusion of space and hallways. A room of about 600 square feet existed in secrecy. It could not be accessed on the same level. A series of doors on different levels led to a hidden elevator that came up through the floor into the room. The elevator did not have a button to rise to the secret room. A panel had to be opened and a code pressed to access the top floor.

Inside was a vast array of high technology that could track ships and planes. Hackers worked 24/7 to intercept messages of law enforcement. This was the brains of a direct link with the cartel headquarters located on an island off Australia.

Syed's ship had become a thorn to the cartel. They controlled the warehouse operation and were privy to all international manifestos. Syed's ship was carrying a valuable shipment from a miner in Australia. That shipment and possibly papers from the pirate ship were with Syed's ship. The plan was to plant plastic explosives to the sides of the ship, get the cargo off, and sink the ship.

The cargo would be directed toward the warehouse, but diverted before it arrived. Simultaneously with the bombing of Syed's ship, the warehouse would be burned. All the evidence of cartel operations would be destroyed with the fire, which would be uncontrollable with the explosives that had been strategically placed throughout the entire complex.

They needed their plan to work or the international cartel bosses would be making ruthless decisions about leadership in the United States. They did not intend to fail.

SIXTY

Captain Syed received a coded message to delay arrival in the harbor. They passed through the Panama Canal and anchored off Cartagena. Guards were posted, but men were allowed to relax, play some games on deck, or fish over the rail.

They anchored at Volcanic Drop with depths of up to 1,000 feet. Blue tuna and barracuda were running. Sailors were thrilled to bring in a large catch.

The four Kachin men from the pirate ship were skilled in filleting the fish. Dinner for two nights was a chef's delight. Hundreds of pounds of fish were prepared for the ship's freezer.

After midnight, all lights above water were turned off. From inside the command center Captain Syed used radar and satellite to ensure they avoided other ships. The engines hummed barely above idle. Miles from point of anchor, speed was increased.

Radar did not indicate other ships in the area. Gradually, deck lights were turned on. Course and speed were set for the harbor docking at midnight in New York City as per instructions from Stewart.

What Syed did not know was that the mystery ship that he had shot and damaged the rudder had been repaired and sailed ahead of him while they were fishing off Cartagena. He also did not know the cartel was tracking by satellite.

SIXTY-ONE

Stewart wanted to meet with Captain Syed and the gold miner when the ship arrived. Alaina was resistant, but Stewart insisted.

He was a British citizen on foreign soil, but his desire to find his son had become consuming. His normal caution had given way to risk-taking. Family enterprises were also at risk. Based on evidence they had received, he was sure his son had once been in the warehouse.

As a British soldier, he had served with MKSP, similar to Special Ops of the United States. Stewart had been reviewing his training. He wanted to be on the side of the law, but he could not ignore the airport bombing and the fact that there were bad people involved.

He had managed to get three former U.S. Special Forces soldiers to be hired as warehouse employees. One of the three was a computer whiz. It had not taken long to tap into the networks and learn that the building was bugged by the FBI. An RS jammer was installed that would be able to frustrate FBI surveillance for a limited time.

What was more important, Stewart's man hacked the system that mapped the route to a secret operations room for the cartel, which was information that he believed the FBI did not have.

Stewart employed three former Navy Seals. One was to stay with Stewart at all times. Two were to be in the water when Syed's ship came in. Twenty-five million dollars does not travel silently.

Azian insisted he accompany Stewart. It was a long discussion with strong opinions. Azian won.

SIXTY-TWO

The four Kachin men who had been rescued from the pirate ship had won the favor and confidence of the crew. Though they looked different from the crew, still spoke their native language when among themselves, and still bowed their heads and mumbled before eating, they were no longer strangers to the rest of the crew.

One of them was skilled in small arms weapons. He had asked Captain Syed to allow him to train all crew in defense. After leaving Australia, there had been daily training. By night they did search and rescue missions on the ship. Defense and offense were rehearsed. By the time they arrived in New York harbor, every man was a tactical weapon.

Syed had received information to tune to a certain frequency. The ex-Navy Seals were in the water and would be able to alert him to any potential danger.

The engines were turned to idle when Syed received a communication that unknown divers were in the water and approaching the ship. Syed instructed the Seals to get at least 50 yards away from his ship. He gave them 60 seconds.

Two ribs of stainless steel pipe wrapped around the entire ship underneath the water. There were thousands of holes in the pipe. The suspicion was that divers were preparing to attach explosives to the sides of Syed's ship.

Sixty seconds ticked by to give the Seals time to be out of danger. Captain Syed pressed a button. Compressed air shot through the holes of the pipes at 5,000 PSI.

Oxygen masks and hoses of the two divers preparing to plant plastic explosives against the ship were ripped into shreds. Frantically and with weakened bodies, they released their packages of explosives in an effort to rise to the surface for oxygen.

The Seals looked for two distressed divers. The action was silent, quick, and lethal.

An "All Clear" signal was given to Captain Syed. Two crewmen accompanying Captain Syed carried the suitcases down the gangplank to where dock workers were waiting with a truck. A Kachin walked with them carrying an AK-47.

Waiting on the dock were Stewart, Azian, and a Seal. Workers further down the dock took no notice of them, thinking they were waiting for a different ship.

The doors to a Mercedes SUV opened. The crewman without hesitation placed the two suitcases inside the SUV. The doors were closed. The Kachin and crewman ran back up the gangplank which was being detached from the ship as they ran. They leaped through the air and rolled onto the deck of the ship.

The ship's engines had never been turned off. Instructions had been given to the first mate to take the ship out about 20 miles and anchor. Port authorities would be coming to investigate, but happenings on the shore would serve as explanation.

The rest of the cargo was worthless—only empty boxes that had been added to the ship to give an appearance of normality. They had used forklifts to create an illusion of an extra-heavy load in the event anyone was watching.

The warehouse workers from the cartel realized their plan had gone wrong. Nothing had happened to the ship after the captain came ashore. There was an attempt at words which quickly turned into anger. Guns seemed to appear out of nowhere.

The action by the cartel was anticipated. The objective was to prevent gunfire, keep the conflict to seconds, and hopefully delay the arrival of shore patrol.

A Seal ripped a weapon from the hands of a man and with a blow to the side of his head left him unconscious. Stewart left a man's arm broken below his elbow, with a gun dropping to the ground. Captain Syed had dealt with many an angry sailor. It only took seconds to have his opponent in a choke hold that stripped him of all rights and property.

One man ran. Azian sent a knife with deadly accuracy, leaving the man alive but incapacitated.

Less than a minute later, all four men were placed inside the Mercedes SUV. They would not die, but it would take more than a few days to recover.

They were taken to an empty building nearby. The four men in underwear were placed inside the building, bound, and gagged. Alaina was phoned. She would use a motel phone in one hour to call for medical help for the injured men.

Azian, Stewart, the Seal, and the Kachin changed into the dock workers' clothes. Captain Syed was expected to accompany the cargo. He remained in full-dress uniform. They took the passes of the warehouse workers to allow them through the gate.

The suitcases from Syed's ship were placed in a waiting SUV along with the clothes of Stewart, the Seal, the Kachin, and Azian. A driver was waiting. As soon as the warehouse truck was gone, the SUV would follow to meet the Australian miner outside the warehouse.

Captain Syed was expected to accompany the cargo and personally deliver the suitcases.

The four men climbed into the dock truck and headed for the warehouse. The SUV followed.

The guards at the gate to the warehouse were not friendly. While they did not know who was supposed to be driving the truck, they thought it was supposed to be loaded. The passes were valid, but something was wrong.

Words were hot and angry. The Seal knew their language. He insisted that dock authorities would not allow cargo off the ship until daylight.

"Apparently, there is some kind of investigation going on. However, the captain has a meeting at 2 a.m. with warehouse officials."

Syed, Azian, and the Kachin were hidden in the back of the truck prepared for action. Fortunately, the guards yielded. The veiled threat worked. They were allowed through the gate toward the warehouse. It was 1:45 a.m.

Minutes later, one of the Seals working in the warehouse area reported to the guardhouse at the gate as crew chief for the next shift. The SUV was waved through without being stopped.

SIXTY-THREE

After dinner in the mansion, full preparations were being made to arrive at the warehouse precisely at 2 a.m. Preacherman had every intention of picking up the assets that had been shipped from Australia. Gold, precious stones, and cash were in those suitcases. He knew that if the cartel took possession, the money would be offshore before daylight.

Preacherman, Trouble, and one of the Navajos rubbed walnut juice on areas of their bodies that would be exposed. They repeated the process several times to get the darkest shade possible.

They dressed totally in black and carried night-vision goggles.

Trouble was ready to take the elevator to the tunnel exit. He stood in front of a mirror looking at himself. He reflected that his mother was dead; and since her death, he had lived in tunnels, culverts, and secret places.

His father might be alive. He was a Navajo brave. He was adopted and living in a mansion with a woman dedicating herself to his care.

He had lived poor. He was living rich. What did it all mean? How had he come to this moment with bad people determined to get their hands on him? Why had his life become intertwined with good people and bad people and mysteries that seemed to have no conclusion?

He reminded himself of his mother's tender words: "Always look for good in people; believe that good will always prevail; believe that it is better to be poor and honest than to be rich and dishonest; and that it is better to be generous than to be selfish."

Would he be alive tomorrow? What would his future be? Where was his father? Where was his mother's family?

He had created a secret place in his room. Opening it, he took out the chain with the medallion his mother had given him and looked at it with a million thoughts going through his mind. He remembered that his mother had told him it was a secret symbol known only by members of his father's family.

Trouble eased the chain around his neck and felt the emblem slide down as if into his heart. The feeling of the medallion against his body gave him hope. Hope that he would be alive tomorrow. Hope that he would one day find his dad.

He took the elevator to the tunnel entrance. He and Preacherman were to make it to the speedboat and meet the Navajo who would drive the truck. With perfect timing, they cruised the river and pulled into a rented boathouse. The gas tank was quickly filled just in case it would be needed when they returned.

Preacherman and Trouble exited the boathouse, padlocked the doors, and climbed into the truck. The Navajo driver observed all speed limits and traffic signs. It would not be wise to be stopped with their faces stained and wearing black clothes. If the truck were to be inspected, weapons charges would make San Quentin look like a picnic.

They approached the gate of the warehouse. A Seal walked out to meet them, pretended to look at the papers they showed him. He looked inside the truck, talked with them and waved them on.

The Seal went back inside and found that two guards had become unconscious with the drugs he had put in their coffee. They would awaken tomorrow with absolutely no memory of what was about to happen. He left the gates unlocked with a chain loosely holding them together and made his way toward the warehouse building. He had only a few minutes to take a few more guards out of commission. They would wake up with headaches. He signaled for the jammer to shut down FBI surveillance.

At 1:59 a.m., the SUV and the warehouse truck pulled into a parking space near the main entrance of the warehouse building. Two Seals had taken up safe positions where they could see the front and back of the warehouse. One of them was monitoring conversations inside the secret room. He was communicating developments with Stewart.

Instructions had just come down from cartel bosses not to leave Captain Syed or any of the men with him alive. Best to leave no witnesses and create an alibi, even though they assumed the men with Captain Syed were their own.

At exactly 2 a.m., the black truck arrived. Preacherman stepped out to meet Captain Syed. While the suitcases were transferred to a sealed compartment of the truck, the Navajo kept the truck engine running.

Floodlights came on bathing the area. With instant precision, the Seals and the Kachin eliminated every light in seconds.

All hell broke loose. Bullets were flying. Preacherman yelled to Stewart, Syed, the Kachin, and Azian to get inside the truck. The Navajo driver was ready.

Pings of bullets were hitting the steel exterior of the truck while it was in a mean arc at high speed. Preacherman uttered a Navajo word. A grid of steel pipes extended from the front of the truck and rose up to about 7 feet high and wider than the truck.

They hurtled through the wall of the warehouse into a vacant area as had been planned. Counting on the element of surprise, the Kachin and Captain Syed ran behind a block wall and up some steps to take positions where they could see most of the ground floor.

Preacherman had given Syed an Uzi with plenty of ammunition.

Trouble used darts to disable two men. He threw a non-returning boomerang that sliced into a spotlight fed by a generator.

Stewart's plan was for him and a Seal to get to the secret communications room.

The Navajo driver was talking his language. A grenade launcher came up out of a secret compartment in the rear of the truck. Three launches later, the vehicles of the bad guys were rubble.

Alarms had been silenced by one of the Seals. Only a few dim lights survived inside the building. Minutes counted like an eternity. They did not have an eternity. Police would soon be coming. The action needed to come to closure.

Stewart and the Seal were following the map toward the secret room. According to the map, the only access inside the room was an elevator. Pressing the elevator button, the doors opened. Men with guns faced them. It was a hopeless situation.

They dropped their weapons. Hands bound behind them they were forced to march in front. Death seemed certain.

A yell into the dimly lighted warehouse announced they had two captives, one British and one American. They would kill their hostages unless they were allowed to exit.

All action stopped. Only one bulb was still shining, and it was low wattage. Trouble put on night-vision goggles.

Stewart and the Seal could be seen with a man behind each of them. It was apparent that Stewart and the Seal were in pain. There was no sound. No motion—other than the shuffle of feet.

When they were about 25 yards from the black truck, there was a pause. Apparently frightened, the man behind Stewart meant to shove him, but instead stabbed him. Stewart fell hard against the floor. Blood oozed from his body.

Trouble was poised and steadied; he instantly loosed an arrow. It pierced the shoulder of the man who had injured Stewart. Preacherman had a laser beam on the man behind the Seal. The Seal seemed to have a sixth sense of what was happening and whipped his body around. Trouble's second arrow found its mark on the red dot of the laser.

The Kachin had taken a position in the ceiling. He dropped from behind with an AK-47 and left no argument.

The Seal picked up Stewart and ran toward the truck. Trouble, Azian, and Syed jumped into the truck as it was moving.

The Navajo had already turned the truck around. The Seals left behind had a few things to do before disappearing.

The truck went back out the hole it had made to enter. The steel bars retreated. Fifty yards away, Preacherman pressed a timer that would give the Seals two minutes to do what they had to do and be clear.

Plastic explosives strategically placed by the Seals in sequence began on the top floor of the warehouse near the communications room. The seventh explosion caused the roof to collapse. Fires were raging. The explosives planted by the cartel were small stuff, but they helped to create an inferno.

The bumper of the truck knocked the gates open. An FBI helicopter moved over the area with camera rolling. The truck was photographed, but the glare of flames against the black vehicle covered with dust from the explosions left it nondescript.

Pictures would not matter. Tomorrow the truck would have a remake, be painted a bright color, and have a chauffeur driving for a rich Australian.

Inside the truck, curtains were pulled to seal off the back. Captain Syed had treated many an injured sailor. He took charge.

Stewart was turned on his side. In minutes, the wound was bandaged. Stitches and additional treatment would come later. The hemorrhaging was stopped.

Trouble took note of the Kachin with his head bowed and mumbling words that sounded a lot like prayer. He had seen his mother like that and thought she was talking to herself. When he would question her, she would say:

"I am on a journey from where I used to be in my father's family to a new place your dad told me about. It is still so new. I promise when I understand better, I will tell you about this journey."

Stewart lay on his back. He had lost a lot of blood. The soiled shirt was removed to bathe his chest.

Trouble gasped. There was a medallion on Stewart's chest. He lifted it and studied it carefully. Then he retrieved the one from his chest. There was no question: the medallions were identical!

Stewart was losing consciousness when Trouble leaned over and held the two medallions close enough for him to see.

Stewart looked at the two metals and the face stained with walnut juice, and then whispered: "What is your name?"

"Sir Walter Scott," Trouble said.

"I will live, son. I will live," Stewart whispered as he slipped into unconsciousness. He had found a piece of Rahel.

Syed and Preacherman heard the whispered voice. It was not closure, but an opening chapter.

CONTACT AND PURCHASE INFORMATION

Order *Trouble* and *Double Trouble* @ BaresEyeView.com

The third novel in the series is to be released in 2019.

Trouble: $14.95

Double Trouble: $14.95

Follow the adventures of Trouble on Facebook @ BaresEyeView

If you have questions, comments, or would like to leave a review, please contact us @

Facebook.com/BaresEyeView
and
Trouble@BaresEyeView.com

Other books authored by Dr. Harold Bare and available for purchase on our website include:

Hell Is War
A Month of Sundays
Trouble
Double Trouble

www.BaresEyeView.com

Trouble—The Adventures of Trouble
www.bareseyeview.com

TROUBLE is a mystery adventure of an orphan boy living in the streets of New York City. His uncanny prowess and natural "Holmesian" ability to sleuth out trouble drive him on a journey across the United States, alongside a Native American/Vietnam War hero who befriends him.